PRAIS

"If you've never read a Vivian Arend book you are missing out on one of the best contemporary authors writing today."
~ *Book Reading Gals*

"LET IT RIDE is a charming, sexy and poignant story and I loved it.
~ *Dear Author*

"Brilliant, raw, imaginative, irresistible!!"
~ *Avon Romance*

"This story will keep you reading from the first page to the last one. There is never a dull moment..."
~ *Landy Jimenez*

"HOLY FREAKIN' HELL IS THIS HOT!!!"
~ *Red Hot Plus Blue Reads*

"This was my first Vivian Arend story, and I know I want more! "
~ *Red Hot Plus Blue Reads*

"Vivian Arend takes us on a sensual ride as Mitch and Anna explore her sexuality... From beginning to end this story is very hot and highly entertaining."
~ *Where the Night Kind Roam*

LET IT RIDE

THOMPSON & SONS: BOOK 4

VIVIAN AREND

ALSO BY VIVIAN AREND

Six Pack Ranch
Rocky Mountain Heat
Rocky Mountain Haven
Rocky Mountain Desire
Rocky Mountain Rebel
Rocky Mountain Freedom
Rocky Mountain Romance
Rocky Mountain Retreat
Rocky Mountain Shelter
Rocky Mountain Devil
Rocky Mountain Home

Thompson & Sons
Ride Baby Ride
Rocky Ride
One Sexy Ride
Let It Ride
A Wild Ride

A full list of Vivian's print titles is available on her website
www.vivianarend.com

This is a work of fiction. Names, characters, places, and incidents either are the product of the author's imagination or are used fictitiously, and any resemblance to any persons, living or dead, business establishments, events, or locales is entirely coincidental.

Let It Ride
Copyright © 2015 by Arend Publishing Inc.
Print ISBN: 978-1-989507-04-9
Edited by Anne Scott
Cover Design © Damonza
Proofed by Sharon Muha

All rights reserved. No part of this book may be used or reproduced in any manner whatsoever without written permission except in the case of brief quotations.

CHAPTER 1

November, Rocky Mountain House

Outside the window, enormous snowflakes were snatched by the rising wind and slammed against the pane, leaving a white barrier clinging to the corners. It was pretty, but prettier still because inside the auto shop where she stood it was warm, the scent of rubber and oil strangely cathartic. Combined with the masculine voices in the background, Maggie was at peace and relaxed.

It was a good way to start her holiday.

She turned from the window as the sound of laughter, deep and familiar, rumbled over her. Her husband Cameron stood next to Clay Thompson, the two of them grinning over some shared joke.

Rocky Mountain House had been home years ago. She had so many good memories of growing up in the small town that when her family had moved to Montana after she graduated, she'd always intended to return some day.

Coming back to make a home with Cameron in the foothills of the Alberta Rocky Mountains seemed right.

Clay Thompson had been around back then, although never more than a friend. At one point she'd thought *maybe* they were ready to head down a different road, but life had changed, and they'd grown apart instead of together. Yet as she admired the two solid examples of manhood before her, there was nothing but contentment in her soul.

Her husband dragged a hand through his blond hair as he spoke, biceps flexing under the sturdy cotton shirt he wore. Clay leaned back on the counter behind him, folding rock-solid arms in front of him as he looked down from his massive height, changing the topic as Maggie approached. "You guys should probably hit the road. The weather's not getting any better."

Maggie slipped her hands around Cameron's arm, smiling up at Clay. "As soon as we're past Airdrie, the roads should be clear."

"And there's no way I'm going to miss my mother-in-law's cooking. It's worth however long the drive," Cameron said.

"You just want a second Thanksgiving dinner," Clay taunted.

"You know it," Cameron agreed. "Best thing that ever happened, marrying someone with family in Montana."

Maggie squeezed his arm before releasing him so he could pull on his thick winter coat. "Clay's right—we'd better get going."

"Your car is completely checked over," Clay assured her.

"He put in extra hours to get us ready on time," Cameron shared before accepting Clay's hand and shaking it firmly. "Appreciate it. The next time we play pool, drinks are on me."

Clay chuckled. "Drinks are *always* on you since the loser buys."

The two guys scuffled for a moment, pounding each other on the back the way guys do as Maggie looked on with amusement.

Then Clay offered her a hug, and she stepped into his arms and squeezed him tight. "Tell your sister I'll be in touch once we get back in a week," she reminded him.

"Katy will be waiting," Clay promised. His strong embrace surrounded her briefly before a firm pat on the back directed her straight into Cameron's arms. "Drive safe, and I'll see you both when you get home."

Her husband backed the car out of the Thompson and Son's garage and into the wild weather. Maggie adjusted her seatbelt, glancing out the window at the driving snow. It was coming down so heavily she couldn't see more than the closest shop windows on Main Street.

As soon as he was on the road, Cameron grabbed her hand. "I'm glad we moved to Rocky Mountain House. It's a good place, with good people."

She smiled at him, catching his eye during the brief moment he glanced away from the road. "After four months, it already feels like home."

All of his attention returned to the road ahead of him. "You know what feels like home? Having things to look forward to, like getting back to work with the guys at the station, or—"

"Or going out drinking and playing pool with the Thompson boys?" she teased.

He squeezed her fingers. "Only when you can't play

with me. Because you're always my first choice for favourite thing to do in my spare time."

Whenever he said things like that, she fell in love all over again. "Sweet talker."

"Love you, babe."

"Always and forever," she answered back automatically, a smile lifting her lips. The ritual begun during their time dating hadn't lost any of its charm, not even after being together for eight years, and married for four of them. She turned to stare into the whiteness of the blizzard. "I know something else you're looking forward to. Turkey addict."

"Yup, I like having two Thanksgivings." He pressed his lips to her knuckles before releasing her hand. "Besides, it reminds me I've got an awful lot to be thankful for."

They both did.

Cameron slipped into the slow line of traffic headed toward the main highway that would take them south. Maggie focused on the faintly visible red taillights ahead of them as she fell silent to let him concentrate on the road.

Counting the moments until the weather improved and the trip was over.

CLAY CLOSED the door to the shop, cutting off the swirling wind and icy temperatures. But he stared for a moment at the steel-grey barrier, struggling to put into perspective the strange sensation inside him.

He liked Cameron. He'd been ready to hate the man, but from the first time he'd been introduced to Maggie's husband, there'd been no way to ignore that Cam was more than a decent guy. He was smart, fun to be around and totally head over heels in love with Maggie.

The one woman Clay had always imagined *he'd* been in love with.

Oh, it had been years ago, and part of Clay's memories were based less on fact and more on daydreams he'd had while holding the family together. When his mom had died the summer he turned seventeen, his world had changed. Sweet-talking Maggie into going out with him had been abandoned in favour of dealing with other more dire needs like keeping the garage out of the red.

There were times he'd regretted that decision, yet he'd never seen any other way he could have dealt. Not at that age. Not with his father tipping into the bottle and his younger brothers dealing with the loss in their own destructive ways.

Still, he'd never expected to become good friends with her husband. Funny how the world worked.

Something solid thumped into his butt before clattering to the floor. He picked up the wrench then faced the work floor.

"How long are you going to stand there, dumbass?" his brother Mitch snapped. "Come on, you said you'd help me with this install, and I don't want to be pulling overtime to finish it. I've got places to go and a woman to do."

"Stop bragging," their youngest brother complained.

"What's the matter, Troy? You get shot down?" Mitch taunted as Clay joined him. "I thought the golden boy of the football field never struck out."

Troy made a rude noise accompanied by a gesture that was hastily hidden when their sister popped open the office door and stepped onto the landing above the main shop workspace. "Coffee run. Who wants what?"

Katy made her way down the stairs, pausing to adjust

baby Tanner in the contraption strapped to her chest as final requests were made.

"You can leave the kid with us." Clay suggested. "It's too damn cold to be hauling a baby around."

She raised a brow. "He's wearing a snowsuit, tucked against my body, and I've got a blanket to cover him with. I highly doubt he'll freeze in the two minutes it takes to walk to the coffee shop. Plus, you're all busy."

"We can watch him," Clay insisted, pointing to the playpen tucked into a safe corner of the shop where Tanner had spent time on occasion. It was one of the great parts of running a family business—all of the siblings worked together with their dad, and no one objected to having their nephew around. Although usually he stayed in the office with Katy when she dropped in to deal with administrative tasks.

Katy's fiancé, Gage, strolled over, wiping his hands clean on a rag before leaning in to kiss her then drop a second kiss on his son's forehead. "Stop fussing, Clay. They're fine."

She offered Gage a wink before repeating back their drink requests, then scooting outside. A blast of icy wind cut off instantly as the door slammed shut behind her.

Gage landed a solid smack into Clay's shoulder as he walked past. "Motherhood. I never thought I'd see it on you."

"Shut up," he grumbled at his best friend.

"You have no idea how close Katy is to duct-taping your mouth shut sometimes." Gage rejoined Troy at the car they were working on. "Suggesting she's screwing up and not watching out for Tanner? Your odds of surviving the next family dinner are dropping rapidly."

6

"I just made a comment about it being cold," Clay muttered as he got back to work.

Beside him, Troy and Mitch were bantering back and forth at each other, the good-natured teasing turned to shared memories of some trip where they'd sweet-talked their way into a hockey game. Clay grinned as he reveled in his family, his dad popping his head in from the front desk where he was booking appointments. The only one of them not around was Len who'd been called out earlier for a towing job.

Thompson and Sons garage was doing all right. People of the community trusted them, and after a few rough years, the family was solid. Heck, his little sister had even ended up with his best friend, Gage, although with how wrapped up in each other those two were, Clay had taken to spending a lot more time with Cameron. He had friends, family—life was good.

Yet as he took a wrench to a particularly stubborn bolt, that waver of discontent returned. Maybe it was seeing everyone else enjoying the one thing so obviously lacking in his life.

It wasn't that he begrudged Cam and Maggie, or Gage and Katy. But even his quiet brother Len had found someone—Clay gave a mental laugh. Actually, it was more like Len had finally stopped running. Janey had been around forever, and now she was a part of the family as well.

With all of them except Troy settled down, and his father happier than he'd been in years, Clay could afford to expend more energy on his own behalf. Make more of an effort.

The idea of diving into the dating world made his skin crawl like hearing nails on a blackboard, but he didn't want to be alone forever. He wanted someone who looked at him the way Mitch's fiancée did. He wanted someone he could keep warm on cold winter nights.

He took a deep breath then let it out slowly.

Stupid, really, the way he was hesitating. Besides, it wasn't as if dating was going to be all bad. He liked the ladies, and they pretty much liked him.

Biggest trouble was he already knew every available woman in Rocky Mountain House and wasn't interested in anything long term with any of them. The thought of it made him cringe, but he probably needed to look at one of those online dating sites. Find some fresh blood, as it were.

The door swung open, and Katy returned, snow driven into her toque, the blanket over the baby white with it. Keith Thompson, the family patriarch, popped out of the front room to help carry the coffee down to the floor, pausing to speak quietly with Clay.

"Just took a call from the RCMP. They said there's some major trouble out there. They need an extra tow truck."

Clay grabbed his winter coat and slipped on his oversized outdoor boots. He stole his coffee from the tray, offering Katy a nod of thanks as he answered his father. "No problem. Did they already contact Len?"

"He's working on four cars in the ditch out Shunda Creek way. He'll join you on the main highway when he's done." Keith Thompson's expression grew serious. "Sounds like a pretty horrendous accident."

The warning was well taken.

With the added height of the truck cab, Clay got a prime view of the mess as he rounded the bend to where a dozen sets of flashing lights turned the white sky into a light show. More than one ambulance and more than one police car were out, with dozens of cars slid off the road on either side of the highway.

But it was the site directly in the center of the T-intersection that turned his gut to sheer ice. A southbound semi had slid through the traffic and T-boned a car heading out of Rocky Mountain House.

The Civic was a mess. The driver's side was crumpled beyond belief, the door crushed toward the middle of the car—a far too *familiar* car.

Clay hurried to place the tow truck in position, following the RCMP's swinging glow sticks, while the only thought going through his mind was he had just finished working on a car exactly like that one. He swore it was Cam and Maggie's.

As soon as he could, Clay jumped from the cab, adjusting his coat as he hurried toward the back of the truck to meet the RCMP. The sirens from all but one of the emergency vehicles had paused, but the red and white warning lights continued to flash off and on, lighting the scene like some sick disco ball.

The chill in his stomach changed to outright nausea as he confirmed the crushed vehicle was the one his friends had recently left the shop in.

"Where are the passengers?" he shouted over the wind at the RCMP assisting him.

"First ambulance took the driver. Passenger got loaded into the one that just left." Constable Shacklee shook his head as he helped Clay attach chains to winch the vehicle into position. "We'll be cleaning this up for a while."

Clay went into autodrive, hooking up the vehicle and climbing back into the cab, the storm ringing in his ears even after the doors were closed. He turned on his own warning lights and followed the RCMP back onto the road, but the entire time his brain was fixated on one thing.

He grabbed the walkie-talkie from the dashboard, opening the shop channel. "Clay to home base, come in."

It took a moment before static buzzed briefly. "What's up?" Troy demanded.

"I'm bringing in a car then I need you to take over for me."

Something of his desperation must have come through because his youngest brother failed to tease, a fact for which Clay would be grateful once he was functioning again.

"I'll be ready." Troy promised. "You okay?"

He wasn't sure how to answer that. The urge to drop everything and ambulance chase drove him so frantically he was past the point of making a judgment call. He didn't want to think. Didn't want to reason—all he knew was he had to get to the hospital as fast as possible.

THE HARD PLASTIC waiting-room chair under her hips was cold through her jeans. The bright lights of the hospital hallway shone with a strange hazy glow, breaking into a million rainbows as her gaze bounced from one to the next. Yet there were no rainbows around her right now—only noise and confusion, people bustling past from the emergency room, rolling beds flying by the side hallway as a collection of mothers with snotty-nosed children looked on with wide eyes.

And her. Shuffled out of the examining room after being declared miraculously uninjured but for a few aches and pains from being slapped by the airbag, and a bruise across her chest from the seatbelt. Beyond that, nothing.

Nothing but the ringing in her ears that refused to die, the shrill sound of metal compressing, bright lights blinding her and a low moaning noise that refused to fade.

"Mrs. Ward. Maggie."

A pair of pristine white runners appeared before her. Above them, cotton nurse's scrubs covered with tiny dancing dinosaurs. Maggie lifted her head and gazed into a pair of concerned blue eyes, vaguely familiar ones. She struggled to recall the woman's name. "Yes?"

"Did you want to wait closer to surgery? Where your husband is?" the nurse asked.

Maggie glanced around, confused. "I thought I was waiting in the right place. Is there any word—?"

"No. Not yet, but when you didn't come back from the washroom, I wondered if you'd gotten lost." The nurse helped her to her feet. "Do you remember what happened, Maggie?"

Obviously just because there was nothing physically wrong with her, it didn't mean she was fine. Maggie took the nurse's arm and tried to remember how she'd gotten turned around. "Cameron. Is he okay?"

"He's still in surgery, but we'll check when we get upstairs." The nurse glanced at her. "Did you have a cup of tea yet? Or something to eat?"

Maggie shook her head. Her limbs trembled as they walked slowly down the hallway toward the elevator.

"*Maggie.*"

The call came from behind them, heavy footsteps sounding from the emergency area, and she turned to discover Clay Thompson barreling down on them like an oversized bull.

He reached for her hands. "God, I was so worried. Where's Cam?"

11

The nurse cleared her throat. "I'm taking Maggie back up to the second-floor waiting area. You'll have to stay here."

That sense of ominous foreboding tightened Maggie's hands firmly around Clay's. "He's our friend. I need him beside me. Please," she added, staring into worried blue eyes.

"Please, Tamara," Clay added. "I want to help."

Tamara—that was her name. Tamara Coleman, from their high school days. It seemed to take forever but it was probably only seconds later when she nodded, gesturing them forward. "Follow me."

Clay loosened Maggie's grip, immediately placing his arm around her, guiding her down the hallway. "Are you okay?"

"Yes." An enormous lump was lodged in her throat. "But Cameron..."

He squeezed her. It was he all could do, but for now, it helped.

Everything passed in a blur as they made their way to the small family waiting room off the surgery. Tamara returned and handed her a cup of sweetened tea with the strict order to drink it all. Maggie didn't have the heart to say she wasn't thirsty. She wasn't hungry.

She was scared to death.

"Drink." Clay repeated the order softly as he wrapped her free hand with his. "I'll stay with you."

She nodded and held on tight. "It just happened. No warning, no way to—" Her voice broke as every nightmare she'd ever had swept in and overwhelmed her.

"Shhh, it's okay." Clay twisted to the side, putting aside the cup before pressing her head to his chest, cautiously cradling her. "Cam's a fighter," Clay assured her. "You just wait. I'll stay with you until he's back."

She fisted her fingers in his shirt and held on, tears she refused to let fall filling her eyes. *Cameron was going to be okay, he was going to come back to her. Cameron was going to be okay—*

How long they sat there she had no idea, but by the time the door swung open and a doctor stepped forward, her limbs had stiffened to immobility. Yet even after the shock of the accident, more terror threaded through her veins at his expression.

"Mrs. Ward?"

Clay helped her to her feet. She kept a tight grip on him as she faced the doctor. "Cameron?"

The doctor shook his head. "I'm so sorry. There was nothing we could do."

The bright lights with the rainbow halos blurred together as the knot of tears in her throat rammed downward into her chest, shattering her heart completely.

CHAPTER 2

Maggie listened to the silence.

Her footsteps echoed on the hardwood floor as she walked through the house. Before when Cameron had gone out of town without her, it hadn't felt this lonely because he'd still been there. The signs of him all around—in the book beside his chair, in the dirty plates he insisted on leaving on the counter no matter how many times she'd laughingly demonstrated how to open the dishwasher door.

None of those things were there. Not even his socks, one on the floor, one dangling from the laundry basket as if attempting to make a breakaway and join its partner.

She would've cried except she had no tears left. All she had was a sense of hopelessness, a sense of being lost, and after nearly a month, a moaning in her ears that refused to go away. So like countless days before, Maggie clicked on the television then left the room, methodically working her way through the entire house turning on radios and setting computers to YouTube stations. Anything to fill the emptiness.

She dropped onto the bed and stared at their wedding picture. "I miss you, sweetie," she whispered, "It's hard to get through each day without you."

There was no answer—and she didn't expect one. Not even a voice in her head, because he hadn't spoken since the moment he'd teased her about being afraid on the highway.

She hadn't cleaned out his closet or begun to remove the rest of his things from the house. Right after he died, when there'd been family around who offered to deal with the task, it had been too painful to consider and she hadn't been ready. She *still* wasn't ready, not for that, but it would be Christmas in a few days, and at some point she had to stop ignoring her friends who kept trying to find ways to support her.

Maggie picked up the phone and called Carol.

Her friend's voice rang with honest happiness. "Hey, good to hear from you. How have you been? You need anything?"

Even as guilt hit for avoiding Carol, Maggie brushed it off. Nobody, least of all her friends, expected her to be the life of the party. "I'm okay. Feeling a bit of cabin fever," she confessed. She stood and headed for the kitchen. "Want to go out for lunch today?"

On the other end of the line her friend made a regretful sound. "I have brunch with the in-laws, but why don't you come over for supper?"

Carol's husband was adorable. A really sweet guy, but the two of them had gotten married this summer and were all newlywed lovey-dovey, and Maggie didn't think she could stand it. Not yet.

"That doesn't work for me. I already have plans," she lied smoothly, because it wasn't *really* a lie. She had plans to do something other than watch them be goo-goo eyed over each other.

"The invitation is open for you to join us for Christmas," Carol reminded her. "Honey, I don't want you to be by yourself. You're *always* welcome around here, any time. You know that, right?"

Maggie nodded. She knew she was welcome, but even as she forced herself to move forward, there were some things she couldn't handle. Carol was a friend, but joining them for Christmas just felt...off.

So she redirected the conversation. "When are you free?"

They set up a time after the holidays, and even though it was days away, Maggie felt a bit better once she'd taken that first step.

She took down the calendar and placed it squarely in front of her, pen in hand as she wrote in the lunch date. Five days loomed between then and now, so she gritted her teeth and reached for the phone.

Finding things to fill in the calendar was easier than expected. Between pulling an extra shift at the local food bank and offering to be an extra set of hands in the Baptist Church nursery on Christmas morning, she found a reason to get out of the house at least once a day. The only empty space remaining was Christmas Eve day.

The forgotten phone in her hand rang, surprising her so much she nearly dropped it.

"Hello?"

Clay's deep voice rumbled over the line. "I'm not taking no for an answer," he said.

That reminded her. Maggie paced to the window, glancing outside. Sure enough, her sidewalks had already been shoveled clear of the overnight snowfall. "How'd you sneak over here and get the snow done without me knowing?"

"It's not me," Clay insisted. "I have a bunch of Christmas elves on retainer. They show up every time we get a fresh fall."

In spite of the heaviness of her heart, her lips twitched into a smile. "So, what is it I'm not supposed to say no to?"

"Christmas Eve dinner. Katy wants to know what you plan to bring."

Her first response of denying the invite was cut off by the mention of Katy.

"Damn you, Clay Thompson, for bringing your sister into this." She'd been working with the young woman, tutoring her on remedial math to help her regain the skills she'd lost in an accident. It wasn't the usual work she did, but through it she and Katy had become close. They'd taken a break since Cameron had died, but had remained in contact. "You know I can't say no to her."

"Your point is?"

Her point was she should have expected this from him. Clay had become a bit of an anchor in her life. Someone who was around often enough she'd been unable to sink into absolute wallowing pity for herself and her loss. Still...

"You need to admit you're a menace," she complained lightly.

"If you insist. I'm a menace. You didn't tell me what you're bringing."

Maggie hesitated. "I might not be able to stay the entire evening," she warned.

"And everyone will be perfectly fine with that," Clay conceded. "You say the word and I'll take you home, but you need to do this, Maggie. You need to..."

He didn't say *you need to do it for Cameron's sake*, but the words were there, hovering like always.

Clay was right. Her husband wouldn't have wanted her to become lost in her sorrows, but knowing that and dealing with it were two vastly different things. "I'll bring dinner rolls," Maggie offered. "That sister of yours is constantly teasing for baking."

He lowered his voice. "Just between you and me, it's the one thing she hasn't managed to excel at.

The shared secret lightened Maggie's heart.

"We'll leave at four," he added.

"I can drive myself," Maggie hurried to protest. Then she could leave when she wanted without pulling him from his family.

"No sense in that. I need to look your car over and do an oil change, so I'll be there a little earlier."

"You're not going to do an oil change on my car and then go straight to your family's Christmas party."

"Of course not. I'm going to do an oil change, wash my hands, *then* go to the party."

Maggie rolled her eyes. Arguing with him was like arguing with a brick wall.

So she'd just be more of a brick. "Take care of my car later. No, wait... Why are you taking care of my car here at all? I can bring it to the shop next week."

He grumbled. "The shop is full and it's time for your next oil change. I'm not talking about doing brain surgery before the party. Don't be so stubborn."

Said the brick wall.

Maggie gave up. "Fine, but I'm leaving baking on your truck seat as payment, and you're not allowed to give it away this time."

She got off the phone feeling a little as if she'd been

pulled through a wringer. He was determined to watch over her, and while she appreciated it most of the time, there were moments his attention just made it harder. She understood, though. He was grieving too, and it seemed he gained comfort from providing for her, even if it was shoveling her sidewalks.

Thinking about him and Cameron laughing together was bittersweet.

She glanced down at the table and the empty space on the calendar for December twenty-fourth. "Well, it seems I've completely filled my social calendar. Yippee."

It wasn't exactly happiness she felt as she added the dinner invite to the list of activities, but it was something more than being empty.

It took a moment to work up the courage to get out of his truck and approach Maggie's house. Part of it was the weight Clay felt every time the painful reminder hit that Cameron was no longer there. His laughing, joking friend was gone, and something inside him ached at the loss.

He'd lost his mom, true, but as horrid as that had been, he'd had time to prepare for her death. And then he'd been so busy that grieving had been eaten up by surviving. This was the first time he'd faced the sudden death of a good friend.

But the deeper ache was from the helplessness that rocked him when he looked into Maggie's eyes and saw her pain. Saw it, and was unable to make things better. All he could do was be there for her like he'd promised.

Clay forced himself to do the next thing. He marched up the back steps and rang the bell.

The rich scent of cinnamon and sticky sweetness hit him as she swung open the door, lips curling into a small smile just for him as she stepped back to let him enter.

"It smells good in here," he said, taking a deep appreciative breath. "Cookies?"

"And cinnamon buns. And rolls." She held her hands awkwardly in front of her as if uncertain what to do with them. That ache in his heart twinged again, and he paused in the middle of loosening off his coat. Gloves and toque in one hand, he opened his arms and pulled her in for a quick hug.

A quick hug that grew longer as she slipped her arms around his torso and offered a long, steady squeeze in return before slipping away.

The laughter in her eyes was missing, but her smile was real. "As much as it pains me to say this, thank you for bullying me into going out tonight."

Clay finished removing his coat and boots, then laid a hand over his chest. "Bullying you? Me? Never."

"What you prefer, steamrolling?"

He cleared his throat. "I'd prefer a cinnamon roll, if I can steal one while they're hot."

She crooked a finger at him and led him into the kitchen, the scent of Christmas goodies filling the space. "You want a cup of coffee with that?" she asked.

Clay checked his watch. "If you don't mind me doing your car next week instead."

"I thought it was silly you were going to do it today. Of course." Maggie pulled a chair back from the table and gestured to it. "Relax. It'll just be a minute."

He sat where she'd directed, examining the full tabletop before him. There were a dozen baskets lined with wrapping paper, some of them partially filled with cookies and fruitcake and other tasty offerings. "Are you setting up a bakery?"

"Christmas presents for people I want to say thank you to." She lowered two coffee cups to the counter, her back toward Clay as she worked on their drinks. "So many people have been kind to me. And it's helped distract me—getting the baskets ready."

She spoke easily, but tension held her upper body stiff. There was nothing he could say to lessen her burden, and he was sure she didn't want admiration, so he did the only thing he could.

"Do you need a hand dropping them off? We can do that before we go over to Katy's."

Maggie placed the coffee in front of him, settling in the chair kitty corner to his. "Thanks for the offer, but it's on my calendar for tomorrow."

"Then I'll help you tomorrow," he said. "The shop isn't officially open until next Wednesday."

"I don't want to interrupt your plans—"

"Maggie." Clay grabbed her hand, squeezing her fingers briefly before letting them go. "If you don't want me along, just say you'd like to do it yourself. But I wouldn't offer if I didn't want to help."

She let out a sigh that seemed too big for her body. "I'd love to have your help, but don't bullshit either of us. You know damn well you *would* help me even if it were the last thing you wanted to do. If you thought it was the right thing to do."

Clay took a drink of his coffee to cover up how accurate her words were. "Then it's a good thing I *want* to go for a drive with you tomorrow."

They sat quietly for a moment. Maggie's hands were wrapped around her coffee mug as she stared distractedly at the wedding ring she still wore. Noise drifted around them, and the longer he listened, the more confused he became. "What are we listening to?"

Her cheeks flushed red. "I don't know. It's just background noise."

Another turn of the screw in his heart. He remembered that—how silent the house had become after his mother died. It seemed impossible that with five teenagers in the house, it had been one small woman who had actually filled the place with laughter. With life.

He pushed aside the painful memories and focused on the cooling racks covered with cookies and the pans of cinnamon buns on the stove. "Are you going to feed me before you put me to work, or after?"

Maggie pulled her attention back to him, eyeing the baking as if measuring it up. "How about during? Any cookies that break we get to eat."

"I like the way you think." Clay teased softly. "Is this one of those rules that says cookies made for someone else have no calories? My sister told me about that."

They rose to their feet, and Maggie instructed him how she wanted the remaining goodies placed in the baskets. Clay washed his hands at the kitchen sink then went to work. She vanished for a moment, the sound of chaos in the background fading until only the soft tune of a Christmas carol drifted from the living room.

Maggie offered him a sheepish smile as she reentered the kitchen. "Better?"

"Much better." He popped a shortbread cookie into his mouth, the buttery goodness melting instantly. He offered her a rumble of approval. "I've changed my mind. We're not delivering these baskets tomorrow."

She paused in the middle of fitting cinnamon rolls into a bag. "What?"

Clay shook his head before offering her an evil grin. "I'm pirating the lot of them. They're mine. All mine."

"Grinch."

He didn't answer, just stole another cookie.

By the time they had everything packaged, he'd coaxed a couple more smiles from her. "Are you ready to go?"

"Give me a minute to freshen up." She paced past him, pausing to brush cookie crumbs off his chest. "You need to get cleaned up as well. Come on, you can use the guest room."

He followed her down the hallway. Maggie gestured to one side then carried on, and he paused before entering, watching her take a few more steps before vanishing into the master bedroom. He stepped into the guestroom and leaned back on the wall. Took a deep breath for strength.

Because somewhere in the past hour he'd realized exactly what a sick bastard he was. Even as he grieved for his friend, even knowing how much she was hurting, he couldn't stop thinking about her. Not about her pain and sorrow, but about the soft curves under the flour-dusted apron.

Couldn't stop wanting to reach out and stroke her cheek. Her arms. Her entire body. He wanted to pull her into his embrace and not just comfort her, but make her forget, if only for a little while.

He wanted to taste her cookie-sweetened lips. Hold her hand and be there for her, yes, but the attraction he'd felt so many years ago—the desire he'd forced away when she'd returned to town in the summer? The craving he'd had no right to feel for his friend's wife?

It was back, and he was shocked by the raw strength of it.

The sound of running water in the distance added to his misery, his imagination sending him images of water droplets slicking down her smooth skin. What he wouldn't give to use his tongue and follow the same path. Down her shoulders, over the curve of her breast. Down her belly all the way to her sex. Lingering there until sounds of pleasure escaped her lips.

Clay cupped the iron-hard erection pressing violently against the front of his jeans. His body's extreme reaction wasn't right, especially since they were both still mourning. But he could as soon stop the sun from rising in the morning as stop wanting her.

Steely determination hit. No way would he let her know how screwed up he was. This was his issue, and he'd be damned if she felt even a moment's discomfort around him. As much as he wanted her, he wanted to take care of her even more because *that's* what she needed.

He hurried into the guest washroom and turned on the cold water, sticking his head under the tap. It would've been better if he could have doused his entire body, but the shock helped ease the urgency of his cock. Clay towel-dried his hair, rubbing rapidly until the dark strands stood in all directions as he glanced into the mirror. "I look like a damn hedgehog," he muttered.

He dragged his fingers through it best he could before giving up and straightening everything else.

Maggie's brows rose sharply when she joined him in the living room. "New fashion statement?"

"I need to borrow a comb," he confessed. "Or get a haircut. It's too long for me to leave it."

"Don't cut it," she said over her shoulder, pacing back

toward the bedroom. "Your hair looks good this length. Well, it looks good when it's not acting out violently all over your head."

She was back in a moment, ignoring his outreached hand and tidying his hair herself. He stood stock still, unsuccessfully ordering his body to remain unaffected. Unlike him, she was completely focused on her task, smoothing the sides, reaching up to use her fingers on the hair over his forehead. She smiled with satisfaction as she pulled it into place.

Her gaze lowered to meet his, and there was nothing there but genuine affection and amusement. "There, that's much better."

Clay used every bit of acting ability he had to respond lightly instead of ruining everything by blurting out something inappropriate. Or worse, grabbing hold and kissing her until they were both breathless. "I'm ready to go if you are."

All through getting into the car with the baskets she'd made for Katy and his father, she chatted and he drilled his brain with the command to stay on guard.

Being there for her was the *only* thing he could offer, and he'd damn well better remember that.

CHAPTER 3

Clay pushed open the door and Maggie stepped in ahead of him, entering a world of warmth and heavenly smells.

The room was filled with Thompson family. Coloured lights glittered on the Christmas tree in the corner, and piles of brightly wrapped boxes of all shapes and sizes were stacked under its base. Cheerful pillows and blankets rested in the few empty chairs, or were draped over the back of the couch.

Katy came forward with a smile, reaching to take the basket of goodies. "I'm so glad you came."

"Thanks for inviting me."

Maggie stumbled for a moment on the shoes and boots left scattered at the door before a pair of hands gripped her firmly, holding her as she caught her balance. For a brief moment she was pulled against Clay's hard body while Katy's fiancé sheepishly rushed forward to clear space underfoot.

"Sorry about that," Gage apologized. "This is what

happens when a hoard of family returns to the house they grew up in—we're pretty casual around here."

"No problem."

Clay guided her to a clear spot, and she slipped off her shoes, allowing him to take her coat.

"It's like running an obstacle course every time," he grumbled. "Wall-to-wall clutter."

"Says the man who never throws anything away." Gage offered a hand to his best friend, shaking it firmly as if they hadn't spent most of the week together at the shop. "You have the original packaging for the clock you got the last year of high school."

Maggie glanced over her shoulder surprised to see Clay's cheeks flush red with embarrassment. "Really?"

He placed his hand on her lower back, his touch protective as he guided her into the room. "Ignore him. He's just jealous I can find things when I want."

Gage chuckled and offered them both drinks. Maggie made her request then wove her way to the empty space next to Clay's dad. "Mr. Thompson. Merry Christmas."

He rose to his feet and ignored the hand she offered him, instead folding her in an enormous bear hug. "Merry Christmas, and I'll tell you again, call me Keith."

He pulled away and stared into her face for a moment before nodding. She worried for a moment he'd say something encouraging and her current tear-free mood would vanish, but he simply caught her fingers and squeezed them before settling on the couch and patting the space next to him. "Sit by me. You'll be out of the bedlam and have a good view."

She joined him, grateful the rest of them seemed occupied with whatever they were doing. Clay's brothers lifted their heads and offered waves or nods before going back to their activities, but other than that there was no direct focus placed on her.

Troy was seated on the floor in front of the couch, bent over something. His dark hair fell across his face, nearly as untidy as Clay's had been. She leaned sideways for a better view as she tried to figure out what he held in his hands.

"How long are you going to keep tangling with that before you give up?" Janey asked, the trim, long-legged girl looking up from where she and Len Thompson were wrapping a couple of boxes with bright-red paper.

"I'm not giving up," Troy insisted. "The three pieces are supposed to come apart, and they just..." He caught hold of what looked like a metal pretzel and shook it, the loose pieces clanging against it like a convoluted Christmas bell.

"He's been working on that all afternoon," Keith shared, speaking softly. "Came in a box with a note that said 'bet you can't do it'."

Which would explain Troy's stubborn determination.

Maggie glanced over by the tree where Mitch Thompson sat in a rocking chair, his tiny nephew propped in his lap. They were close enough to the fire Mitch wore nothing more than a black T-shirt emblazed with the family garage logo. The full-sleeve flame tattoos on his arms were clear, especially the one wrapped around the baby's torso holding him upright.

Mitch chatted with Anna as she put another log on the fire, Tanner staring around the room with enormously wide eyes as if soaking it all in.

Christmas music played in the background, and Clay's laugh rumbled as he and Katy stepped from the kitchen with plates of food in their hands. Gage rushed forward to clear space on the coffee table, Keith got up and headed toward the table with the drinks.

The entire place buzzed with motion and energy, and Maggie found herself smiling in spite of the cold spot that was ever-present in her heart.

When the cushion beside her dipped, she turned with a light heart to ask Keith a question, stopping with a jerk as she looked into Clay's deep brown eyes. "Oh."

He held out a glass. "Your eggnog."

She grasped it eagerly to cover her momentary unease. Balancing the cool concoction gave her something to concentrate on.

Keith was at the front door, pulling on his coat as he excused himself. "I forgot to bring a couple things. I'll be back in a minute or two."

Clay halfway rose to his feet. "I'll run over to your apartment and grab them."

His dad waved him off. "I can do it. You sit and visit."

Keith closed the door, and the conversation picked up as the siblings gathered around the coffee table.

"I am not a Grinch about Christmas," Anna retorted in defense. "You've been working on that puzzle for too long, Troy, it's affecting your brain."

He didn't bother to look up, focused on unhooking the metal pieces. "I heard you told old Mr. Pfeiffer to turn off his lights."

Anna rolled her eyes. "Where'd you hear that?"

"Down at Traders. The old-timers were talking about it last night, how the RCMP pulled up in front of his house and got all up in his business. He was quite outraged."

A burst of laughter escaped Mitch. Little Tanner tilted his head back and stared at him, mouth hanging open. His uncle gave his nose a pinch before explaining his amusement.

"I bet Pfeiffer didn't mention Anna told him to turn off

one section of lights because the crazy old man had arranged the lines up and down his weeping willow so perfectly that when he flipped the switch, it looked like a giant penis had sprouted in his front yard."

Laughter rumbled across the room. Janey pressed a hand over her mouth to hide a smile, and Katy leaned against Gage's side, the two of them shaking with amusement.

Even Troy gave up on his puzzle momentarily, snickering loudly. "Well, that does change things."

"What did you say to him, Anna?" Katy dropped to her knees on the other side of the table and picked up a sugar cookie, raising it in a toast to Maggie before popping it in her mouth.

"It was one of the most awkward conversations ever. Excuse me, sir, but you seem to have a giant phallic symbol on your front lawn. You might want to rethink your decorating scheme."

Len grinned. "Wonder what the congregation at the Presbyterian Church across the street thought?"

"It didn't fit very well with their nativity scene." Anna shook her head. "Of course, that's how we found out. Pfeiffer turned on the lights right when they were coming out of Saturday evening service."

"Somebody got an eyeful," Janey commented, which just resulted in more laughter from the entire group. She rested her fists on her hips and glared at Len who was snickering the loudest. "Bunch of dirty minds, every single one of you."

Maggie listened to the continuing chatter and felt included without obligation.

Eventually Gage slipped across the room and offered the dinner bell to his son who gripped it with a tiny hand

and shook it vigorously, eyes widening in surprise at the loud noise.

"Dinner." Katy and Janey together gestured them into the kitchen area.

"And I promise no one's getting food poisoning this year," Katy added.

Maggie leaned briefly against Clay's solid side to get his attention as they stood in line to go through the narrow doorway. "Is food poisoning a typical part of your Christmas tradition, and if it is, shouldn't you have warned me?"

He leaned down, his cheek brushing hers as he whispered in her ear. "Standing joke. The first time Katy cooked a turkey she didn't know the giblets and the rest were tucked inside the body. Things kind of went downhill from there."

The house was small enough Maggie expected they would fill plates and return to the living room, balancing their meals on their laps.

She stepped through the doorway amazed to see an addition had been built on the back of the house, with floor-to-ceiling windows that would allow light to spill into the room. A long, trestle table with more than enough room for the crowd of people present sat in the middle of the space, tall tapered candles and holly greens decorating the centerpiece.

"This is beautiful." She turned to Katy in surprise. "I didn't know you were adding onto the house."

Katy elbowed her best friend in the side. "Since Handy Gal here decided to stick around town, I put her to work. Just finished last week."

Maggie nodded in approval. "Great timing, and this is such a wonderful idea. The dining room in our house is far too small. Cameron always said when we started reno-vations..."

The words faded as she remembered there would be no renovations. She'd never see Cameron smile with pride as he welcomed friends around *their* Christmas table.

She swallowed hard then forced herself to pretend nothing was wrong. Fighting away the tears that could over-whelm her far too quickly. "I bet it's very bright in here."

Katy kindly went along with the abrupt change in topic. "One of the best parts of my day is sitting at the table in the morning with a cup of coffee."

Maggie took her place feeling a little more fragile than she had only moments earlier. Determined to stick it out, though, since that's what Cameron would've wanted.

THE GIRLS HAD OUTDONE THEMSELVES. Clay put another scoop of stuffing on his plate before offering Maggie the nearly empty bowl. "Last chance."

She shook her head. "It's delicious, but I'm full."

Clay didn't say anything, but all his warning buzzers went off. She'd barely eaten anything.

Katy caught his eye from across the table, shaking her head slightly before she slapped Troy's fingers as he reached in front of her. "Mind your manners," she warned. "You want your nephew to grow up copying you?"

Troy shrugged as he nabbed the bowl of potatoes from under Mitch's fingers. "Sure. Means he'll be handsome, talented, and able to charm the birds out of the trees."

"And humble," Len muttered. "You forgot that part."

"But of course. *That* goes without saying." Troy glanced

at his third plateful of food and sighed happily. "I don't know why we don't do this every week."

The boys took turns teasing him as the meal pulled to a close, but Clay was more interested in the woman at his side than in taunting his youngest brother.

Maggie had grown quieter as the meal progressed, and Clay stayed alert for the first sign the gathering had become too much for her. But every time he was ready to suggest they leave, she seemed to rally. Adding a small quip to the conversation, or asking one of the girls for a recipe.

Only when Katy told everyone to return to the living room, and they'd have coffee and dessert there, Clay knew it was time. He laid a hand on Maggie's thigh, holding her in place as the rest of the family left the room. He leaned close to whisper in her ear. "You want dessert? Or have you had enough?"

Her shaky exhale let him know he was right. "If you don't mind, I'd like to leave."

"No one minds," he assured her.

He stood and smiled at Katy and her best friend. "You girls did a great job, but it's time I took Maggie home."

"What?" Janey joked. "You're leaving before you devastate the apple pies? What is this world coming to?"

Maggie was at his side as they moved forward, answered quietly, "It's been wonderful, but I'm...done."

Katy pushed her friend aside and gave her a dirty look. "You are such a brat. You know we made them dessert to go."

"You made? Try *I* did," Janey interrupted with a grin as she grabbed a bag off the counter and held it to Maggie. "That guarantees it's edible, by the way. Katy's getting to be a better cook, but adding in her math problems, when she grabs the salt instead of sugar, ain't nobody who wants to try her custard."

"You said you wouldn't tell anyone about that," Katy complained.

Maggie offered Katy a hug. "Well, everything was delicious, and I'm glad I joined you."

"Anytime." Katy wrinkled her nose. She briefly poked her head into the noise-filled front room before popping back with a suggestion. "You guys want to sneak out the back way?"

Clay could sense Maggie was intrigued by that idea, especially when Janey returned to the kitchen with their coats in her hands.

"I should say goodbye to everyone," Maggie spoke softly, hesitation sneaking in.

Janey waved a hand. "Don't worry about it. Everyone enjoyed seeing you. We're glad you came."

"And, Clay, we're opening presents at eleven tomorrow morning. Don't be late," Katy said before she slapped her hand against her forehead. "What am I saying? Of course you won't be late. You're *I'm always there early* Thompson."

Clay tweaked her nose much like Mitch had done to Tanner earlier in the evening. "Thanks for the great dinner, sis, and I'll see you in the morning."

He helped Maggie down the back stairs and around the side of the house.

They were nearly to her house before she spoke. "I should've taken my own car. You didn't need to leave the party yet."

"Oh, yes, I did." Clay said, his relief showing. "Every Christmas Eve after dinner Katy comes up with a new way to torment us all. Gage let it slip that she got a karaoke machine that hooks to the TV, and she's planning on putting everyone into teams and making them sing for the rest of the evening."

"Oh dear. I can see why you didn't want to stay."

Some of the tension had drained out of her, even a touch of amusement back in her voice. Clay acted affronted. "Hey, is that a comment about my singing ability?"

She twisted in her seat to face him. "Yes."

Clay chuckled. "How often have you heard me sing?"

"When you're sober?"

He pulled into the driveway in front of her house. "I resent that statement. That makes it sound like I was always drunk around your place."

"Not at all. But the few times you and Cameron tied one on..."

They sat in silence for a moment. Cam was gone, and damn it, Clay missed him.

He pushed open the door and walked around to help her out, pausing with his hands on top of the door because he had to say something. Had to turn this from a moment where they'd both end up focusing on what they'd lost instead of what they had—great memories of a special man. "You're right. Cam was terrible when it came to taunting me into making a fool of myself. Every single time he managed to pull one over on me."

Her feet slipped on the skiff of fresh snow on the driveway, and he tightened his grip, slipping his arm around her waist as he walked toward the back door. "You were his favourite person to play practical jokes on," she admitted.

He walked all the way in, not hesitating when she suggested he join her for a drink. "I made you miss your apple pie, you should share mine."

"I didn't have the heart to tease Janey. That apple-pie incident that she referred to?" Clay followed Maggie into the kitchen and helped her gather plates. "The winter after Mom died, the girls decided to hold a bake sale to raise money for Christmas shopping, and back then neither of them were very good cooks. I snuck a piece from one of the pies and realized they'd forgotten to core the apples."

Maggie glanced at him in confusion.

"There were stems and seeds in the filling—either people were going to complain or not buy, so I pretended to eat them."

"*Them?*"

"Four pies."

A burst of laughter escaped. "And they believed you?"

"I was seventeen. It wasn't outside the realm of possibilities, so yeah. Once I offered to pay for them all, they stopped complaining."

"And they've never figured it out, what you did?" Maggie smiled as he shook his head. "You're a good big brother."

Clay shrugged. "I did make sure that by the following year they knew what they were doing."

He glanced around the house as she went to grab coffees, bringing them back to the living room. Everything seemed the same as a month earlier—before Cameron had died. But everything had changed drastically.

He wanted to protect her. Wanted to help her deal with all the painful things that were still coming, but he wasn't sure how to even make the offer without hurting her further. And he had to be extra careful now that he had to hide the less than "just friends" feelings he was experiencing.

She seemed so delicate in some ways, yet so strong. Determined to make it through even though she was nowhere near done crying. He'd seen it, especially in the seconds after she'd smile or laugh. The way her amusement would fade and sorrow filled her eyes.

He knew that sensation far too well—the rush of guilt for having a good time before remembering his mom was gone. Feeling guilty now for wanting more than to simply comfort Maggie.

He glanced across the two feet separating them as she lifted the cup to her lips. She closed her eyes as she swallowed the warm liquid, another long sigh escaping her as if it had been an exhausting evening.

"How can I be there for you?" He spoke softly, but her lashes fluttered up, and their gazes met. "What do you need me to do to help you?"

Because not helping her was out of the question.

Maggie put her cup on the table, shaking her head slightly. "I'm okay. There's nothing—"

He closed the distance between them, slipping his fingers around hers. With his other hand he cupped her chin and lifted her face to his. "I know you'll be okay. But that's not answering the question. I'm here for you. Just like I told you at the start, just like I'll always be."

For one terrible moment he thought she would refuse to answer him, then she dipped her chin, her eyes filled with moisture she refused to let fall. "I need a hug."

"That I can do." He wrapped his arms around her so her head rested against his chest. He stroked her hair and held on as she slipped her hands around his body.

Everything about her was soft and warm, and he wasn't strong enough to ignore the scent of her shampoo. Green apples, or something equally wholesome, but the thoughts rolling through him had as much to do with easing her burdens as with helping her forget.

They sat there for endless minutes, silence in the background except for the clock on the wall. An old grandfather clock with two long cords weighted down with metal acorns. The pendulum shaped like a bird on a swinging wire swayed back and forth—producing a constant ticking that echoed through the house.

A low shuddering breath escaped her as she tilted her face toward him. "What am I doing?" she whispered.

"You're getting through one day at a time." Clay gave in and stroked her cheek, wiping away the single tear that had rolled free. "One day at a time."

Maggie shook her head. "Sometimes I walk into a room and I totally forget he won't be there. And every time it happens it's as if I lose him all over again."

He nodded his understanding even as he ached for her. And the decision he'd made to keep his desire under wraps became even more vital. She didn't need a lover—she needed a friend. If it killed him, that's all she would ever suspect him to be.

"He's always going to be a part of you," Clay promised her.

And he held her for as long as she needed him to, pushing his needs aside. Taking comfort from her as well. Dousing the fire in his body and focusing on how much he cared for her in his heart.

Because that's what he did—and that's who he was.

CHAPTER 4

Every holiday was like a fresh blow, but somehow she kept moving.

For New Year's Eve, Maggie insisted she wanted a quiet night at home, and eventually her friends gave in, though concern shone in their eyes.

Her coworkers called to wish her the best. And Clay...

...dropped by the house just as she'd secretly suspected he would.

He had both hands tucked behind his back when she opened the door. "What's up?" she asked.

"I know you said not to stop by, but someone really wants to spend New Years with you."

One hand came out with a stuffed Eeyore in it, the familiar sad eyes and droopy ears bringing a smile to her face. "He's lovely."

Clay pulled his other arm forward and offered her a tub of Ben & Jerry's. An extra-large spoon was tied to the container with a ribbon that matched the one around Eeyore's neck. Clay's expression as he handed them over was so adorable Maggie laughed, sneaking in close to offer him a hug.

"Have a good time at the party with your friends and family," she offered earnestly.

"You're welcome to join us," he reminded her.

She shook her head, lifting the stuffed animal in the air. "I've already got my date for the night. Thank you so much."

He brushed his knuckles over her cheek. "If you change your mind, even if it's at eleven forty-five, call."

But before the ball dropped, she was in bed. Darkness surrounded her, the sheets cold around her body. There didn't seem to be much to celebrate, and not a lot to look forward to either.

And then the calendar stretched open, blank day after blank day facing her. School started right away which was good, because it gave her something to do other than sit at home alone. She worked quietly, removing snow from the school parking lot, doing mindless maintenance tasks. Her brain seemed wrapped in a thick fog as sleepless nights ran together in a blur.

She opened her door to a knock a couple days later and discovered Janey Watson on her front step.

"Have you got a minute or two?" the young woman asked, her cheeks red from the cold.

"Of course. Come in." Maggie poked her head out the door and took a quick peek at the snow-covered lawn and empty driveway. "Did you walk over?"

Janey opened her coat, gloves held in one hand. "I needed to burn off some of the five million calories I consumed over the holidays. It's not far from your place to mine and Len's."

"Do you want a cup of tea?"

"Love one."

Maggie headed to the kitchen as Janey took off her boots then followed her. "I know what you mean about eating too much. I keep cooking the same size meals as before, and there are too many leftovers crowding my fridge."

She swallowed around the small lump that had formed in her throat and focused instead on the bright-faced girl who'd joined her. She thought back to Christmas and the joy that effortlessly surrounded Janey. "How are things with you and Len?"

"Fab." Janey pulled out a chair and made herself at home. "Of course with how much he talks, the only way I find out he *doesn't* like something is when he goes and redoes it after I'm done."

"That could be handy," Maggie said. "If he doesn't like the way you do laundry..."

Janey laughed. "I never thought of that." She shook her head slightly. "Strange how I've known him forever and yet, here we are, still finding out new things about each other. Sometimes it's frustrating, but we keep trying, and I guess that's the important part."

Maggie placed cups of tea in front of both of them and joined Janey at the table. "When Cameron and I were first married, somebody suggested every year we should learn one new thing. We didn't have to learn it together, but whatever we chose should complement each other. Like photography and scrapbooking, or gardening and cooking."

"That's a neat idea." A thoughtful expression drifted into Janey's eyes. "It ensures you spend time together."

"Exactly. In fact, that's part of how I ended up doing landscaping and yard maintenance—it was something we worked on together the first year after we got married."

Janey took a deep breath. "Speaking of things you were

doing together, that's part of why I came over. Did you know Cameron signed up for the next Habitat for Humanity project?"

Maggie considered for a moment before nodding. "We talked about it before, but so far it had never worked with our jobs, and last year we had the move to Rocky. This was going to be our first year volunteering."

"No pressure, but I need to know if you're still interested in being involved." Janey put her cup on the table. "I saw your name on the list and offered to come and check. If it's too much, just say so, but if you'd like to be involved, we'd love your help."

The thought of all those blank days on the calendar popped to mind too quickly. It wasn't that hard of a decision.

"I see no reason why I can't help. It would be good for me. But Cameron was going to take care of the larger landscape work," Maggie added, "and I'm not as good as him on the bobcat."

"We'll find someone to take care of that stuff," Janey promised. "You just help with the parts that are your speed."

"What about the gala fundraiser? We signed up for that as well."

Janey's nose wrinkled for a moment before she flashed a reassuring smile. "Don't worry. I'll deal with it."

Yet even as they changed to other topics, the fundraiser lingered on Maggie's mind. It wouldn't be easy to find new volunteers this close to the deadline. That was part of the reason the committee had lined up volunteers *last* summer. At this point in the year, everyone was committed to other projects.

She pushed her worries aside as a different topic caught her attention. "That addition you did at Katy's house—are you available for more work?"

"Maybe?" Janey gestured to the window and the fresh snow falling outside, huge flakes that drifted down in gentle spirals. "The weather is slowing us down, and I'd have to check the work list with my partner, but I could get you on the schedule."

"I don't know that I want anything done right away," Maggie admitted. "Just want an idea how much a renovation might cost. If it's even possible."

"Of course." Janey brushed her hands on her thighs as she stood. "Do you want to show me around, or do you want me to come back later? Up to you."

The truth spilled free. "Now that you've dropped in, I don't want to let you go. It's nice to have company."

Like the whirlwind of energy and emotion she was, Janey moved without hesitation. She closed the distance between them, her arms flung wide-open like one of those giant stuffed mascots at a football game. "After that confession, no way you're getting away without a hug."

Maggie accepted it without any complaints.

They spent another half hour looking over the changes needed to the older home. Janey had some great suggestions, and time passed far too quickly.

The young woman was pulling on her coat when all the quiet hours stretching ahead of Maggie flashed to mind, and she spoke on impulse. "You know the gala? Don't worry about finding a replacement. I'll head up the event."

"Are you sure? Because—"

"I'm sure. And I'll ask for help if I need it, but you have enough going on already. It's not fair someone else has to take on another task." She smiled at the other woman. "If I get myself in trouble, I'll shout."

"Don't feel guilty calling for help," Janey insisted. "I know I said I'm busy work wise, but Len is pretty low maintenance, and he's good about helping with all sorts of things. The two of us have your back."

Janey bounced down the stairs, lively enthusiasm in her step as snow puffed up from under her boots. She waved at Maggie as she marched the sidewalk, whistling happily as she went.

Moments after Maggie closed the door, silence flooded the room. It rushed in and wrapped her in an icy grasp, and she sighed in frustration before doing her all-too-familiar route around the house to turn on every electronic device possible.

Maybe getting busy with tasks would help ease the loneliness. Maybe soon she'd be able to keep the cold from invading so quickly.

But tonight she wasn't going to do anything except let the tears come. Tears she'd held back the entire time she and Janey had discussed changes to a home that Cameron would never come back to.

PATHETIC. He was capital-P pathetic. Clay grumbled at himself as he crawled behind the wheel of his truck. He'd shut down the shop barely an hour ago and already he was headed back to work.

Nothing caught his attention at home. Everything on the TV sucked, and he had no hobbies he was working on.

Clay considered stopping by the local pub and seeing if

anyone wanted to shoot some pool, but that option didn't sit very well. The last time he'd played he'd spent the entire time missing Cam.

His tolerance tonight was set to low, and he didn't feel like playing the social games that went on at Traders. The flirting from the ladies, and the bullshit from the guys—all of it good natured, but very much *not* what he was interested in at the moment.

Tension tightened his shoulders and back until they ached, and the urge to take something, or someone, apart was growing stronger. Far better he put in extra hours sweating off his pissy mood at the shop than ending up in a fight just because.

But at the last minute he turned, not into the parking space behind the shop, but down the long driveway that led to the small house where he'd grown up.

He was in a horrible mood? Of course he should crash his buddy's place. Maybe it was a shitty thing to do, but Gage *was* his best friend and that's part of what best friends put up with. And it was a rule that baby sisters had to put up with their big brothers.

He knocked on the back door before pulling it open and sticking his head in. "Is everybody decent?"

Laughter spilled from beyond the kitchen, but no one answered, so Clay let himself in. He rounded the corner into the living room where he discovered not only his sister and his best friend, but Len and Janey as well. Janey had Tanner cradled in her arms as they peered at the coffee table intently.

"Hey, guys."

Gage glanced up from whatever they were examining and rose to his feet. "Hey. What's happening?"

"Nothing. I came over to torment Katy for a while."

Katy didn't even look up, just held a hand in the air with her middle finger raised as she continued to discuss something seriously with Janey.

Gage laughed and patted Clay on the back, bringing him into the center of the room. "You should be nicer to your big brother," he scolded Katy. "He's here especially to see you."

"Whatever it is he wants, no."

Clay winked at his friend as he teased his sister, his foul mood dissipating rapidly. "You're breaking my heart."

"Awww. You need repair supplies? There's a stapler on the desk, or Crazy Glue on the top shelf. Take your pick." Only this time she glanced up at him. "Hey, big bro, we're checking the calendar. You have anything you're committed to early spring? Any dates we need to look out for?"

"Not that I can think of, why?"

"Wedding plans," Janey announced happily before shaking a finger at him. "But you're not allowed to get Gage drunk and ship him off on a bus, or anything." Len didn't say a word, but he appeared to be silently laughing. Janey frowned then poked him in the side with her elbow. "What are you snickering about?"

"Clay wouldn't get Gage drunk," Len said, his tone full of amusement. "He'd duct-tape him to a chair to keep him from being hurt. Maybe pad him with a couple pillows first."

Gage rolled his eyes then faced Clay. "Looks like our wild-oats-sowing managed to fly under the little kids' radar. They have no idea what a badass you are. Well done."

"Your wild-oats-sowing? You can explain in more detail when we're alone." Katy gave him a stern look that turned into a smile as she held the calendar in the air and shook it.

"Excuse me for interrupting, but can we get this figured out before Tanner decides he's been good for far too long, and it's time to play his 'no adults get to talk' game? The one where he makes as much noise as possible screaming at the top of his lungs?"

Gage stole Tanner from Janey, tucking him partway under his arm and holding him like a football. Tanner relaxed, happily drooling on Gage's sleeve, little fists waving in the air like he was cheering.

Gage grinned. "Go ahead, he's fine."

Katy gave him an adoring smile. "You're a good daddy."

"Yada, yada, yada." Janey clapped her hands over her ears briefly. "You two are so sickeningly sweet sometimes. Let's arrange to get you married so you can legally annoy people with how cute you are. Pick a date."

"Not Valentine's Day," Katy said.

"Before the summer," Gage added. "I don't want to wait that long."

Janey made another gagging noise that turned into shrieks of laughter as Len tickled her. "Stop it, or I'll sit on you."

Clay was in the middle of happy bedlam, and the last of his tension slipped away. He got down on the floor beside his sister to check the calendar with her. "Smart move, not using Valentine's Day. Everything will be booked already."

"I want Gage to have to give me flowers as often as possible, so I'm not doubling up on any of my celebrations." She ran her finger over the calendar pages working forward from that day's date, and backward from the middle of the summer. "Anna and Mitch are getting married sometime in July, or at least that was the plan the last I heard. They're having trouble organizing a date between her work and the Coleman side of things. So what about we split the difference between now and then, and plan for April?"

Janey finally got away from Len's teasing. She remained in the circle of his arms as the two of them stood over the table. "How about March? Then I can tell Maggie I'll be free to help her if she needs anything for the fundraiser gala —that's scheduled for mid-April."

"What event?" Clay asked, glancing up at her.

"The Habitat for Humanity project. Maggie and Cameron were in charge of part of the fundraiser, and she insists she wants to do it. I can give her a hand, but April is probably the earliest I can swing it, but not if you have the wedding then too."

"Still say you're biting off more than you can chew," Len grumbled. "You're gonna do this organizing when? In your nonexistent spare time?"

Janey let out a long sigh. "I know it's going to be busy, but what could I do? She's all alone, but she really wanted to do it."

Clay kicked himself. This was the first he'd heard about it. "Don't worry, I'll talk to Maggie. I've got more than enough time on my hands."

Katy was in the middle of adding notes to the calendar. She whistled innocently as she mumbled loud enough for him to hear, "Don't be so sure about that..."

Gage sat on the coffee table so he could nudge Katy on the shoulder. Tanner reached for the edge of the calendar and promptly stuck it in his mouth. "Okay, spill. That's the third time tonight you or Janey made a comment about how Clay's about to get real busy. What did you two do?"

"It wasn't us," Katy protested. She glanced at Clay, lips curled into a smile even as she looked rather apologetic. "I overheard Troy and Mitch talking at the shop. It seems they signed you up for a dating service."

"The hell? They didn't."

She nodded reluctantly. "And I don't know any more than that, but if you want to take it out on somebody, I think it was Troy's idea."

Clay glanced at Len. "You know anything about this?"

Len shook his head. "Not my thing."

"I'm sure they meant well," Katy offered before wrinkling her nose. "Well, that *and* they were getting quite the kick out of it."

Good grief. Just what he needed. Although he had considered it himself, the idea had been pushed aside what with Cam's death and trying to help Maggie deal with everything. Dating didn't seem important, especially when he added in lingering frustrations regarding his feelings toward a woman who was still in mourning.

Nope. The whole "getting to know you" relationship nightmare was not what he wanted to fool around with right now.

"Thanks for the heads-up," he said. "I need to get the details out of those two assholes so I can shut it down."

"Don't cancel the account right off the bat," Katy suggested. "Maybe this is a good thing. You haven't dated anyone for a while. This might help."

"Clay doesn't need help finding a date," Gage insisted. "Especially not from those two."

Katy shrugged, sliding the calendar away from her son. "Okay, I'll back off, but it's not the most terrible idea they've ever had." She got to her feet and pulled Clay with her toward the kitchen. "Come on, I'll grab snacks, you grab drinks, and we'll play a game of something."

They took turns entertaining Tanner while the other

four played a card game, and it was family and it was comfortable...and the entire time Clay kept thinking about Maggie. How she was sitting alone in an empty house, and his soul ached.

His promise to be there for her taunted him. She deserved so much more than life had handed her lately. Somehow he'd find a way to ease her pain.

CHAPTER 5

Having made the decision to stick with her and Cameron's plans, Maggie set up an appointment with the head coordinator of the Habitat project and got up-to-date information. Talking with Daniel Coleman helped reduce her fears the task would be way too much, while strangely reassuring her this wasn't some kind of busy work being offered her.

Not that she had anything against hard labour. Things were slow at school since her part-time position as grounds maintenance required nothing more at this time of year than for her to keep the walks shoveled and to care for the indoor plants. She already had everything in place to start seedlings for the greenhouse in a couple of months.

The Home Ec and Shop students would take their turns in the greenhouse helping with that task. The practical life skills she got to teach without having to run a full-time class was the icing on a cake.

She slipped into the greenhouse to double-check how many lights she needed to order, and to check the watering system was in working order. Her footsteps echoed back from the distant ceiling in the long, modified Quonset as she moved from one closed-in section to the next, wearing her medium-weight coat and boots to protect her from the cool temperature of the out-of-season greenhouse.

She stepped through the door into the final room and jerked to a stop with a gasp, her heart pounding briefly before she recognized the heavily bundled man standing just inside the entrance door. "God, Clay, you nearly gave me a heart attack."

He balanced two coffee cups in one hand as he pulled the heavy door closed to shut out the freezing temperature. "Sorry. I wanted to see how you're doing."

Maggie glanced at her watch. "Did you sneak away from the shop?"

He beamed, absolutely zero guilt on his face as he offered her a coffee. "Don't tell anyone. They'll just think it's really busy at Tim Hortons."

She laughed and accepted the drink, leading him toward the side of the room. A couple of tall stools that were normally used while transplanting seedlings were tucked under the counter, and she pulled them out so they could sit. "I'm okay. Just getting things ready in here—I'll be heating it up in about a month's time so I can start the seedlings."

He glanced around with interest. "This wasn't here when we were in high school. Sounds like it's a hit with the kids—the gardening and stuff."

"Most of them. Sometimes I get a few who don't think playing in the dirt is very important, but I rarely see any of them complain when we start harvesting vegetables. And I usually catch the complainers snitching strawberries when they think I'm not looking."

His eyes danced with amusement. "It's definitely a good

thing we didn't have this back when I was in school, then. Strawberries—God, they're my favourite."

She smiled at his enthusiasm. "Just let me know, and I'll help you set up your own patch."

He shrugged. "Not much room for that in my yard."

"You'd be surprised," she teased, suddenly delighted with the idea of surprising him with a strawberry pot for his deck. A thank-you for everything he'd done. Once again it was impulse that made her speak. She'd considered asking him but felt terrible for taking up even more of his time. Yet there was something in his eyes that encouraged her to be brave. "I have a favour to ask."

Instant response. "Anything."

She snorted. "Be careful saying that too quickly. You have no idea what I'm about to hook you into."

"Doesn't matter. Anything you need, I'll help."

She took a deep breath and screwed up her courage. "Cameron and I volunteered to help with a project this summer. Habitat for Humanity is cleaning up the old Miller Hall property and building a set of four seniors' residences on the space. The committee said I could get out of it, but I'd really like to keep the commitment. The project was important to Cameron, and I feel as if I need to do this."

Clay nodded slowly. "Kind of like doing it in his memory. To honour him...?"

"Yeah." Her chest ached, tightness binding her briefly before she pushed her grief away. "And while someone else could step up to help me, it would be extra special if you were the one. We could do this together, for him."

He turned away for a moment, and she studied his profile without speaking. There was sadness there, a furrow folding his brow as he stared at the bright calendar on the wall.

January fifteenth. Not even two months had passed since Cameron had died, and another wave of pain washed over her. Clay cleared his throat and seemed to be fighting for words. The two of them momentarily wrapped up in their shared loss.

When he turned back, it was to catch her fingers in his and squeeze them briefly. "I'd be honoured. I'd already heard about the project, and I was going to offer to help, but doing it in his memory? Definitely."

A warm glow lit inside that curled around the constant ache she carried, not just from his agreement, but from the other parts of his comment. She swallowed hard and focused on the fact the rumour mill had gone ahead of her. "Of *course* you've already heard. Why did I think otherwise?"

"You forgot the power of discussing anything with Janey." He shrugged. "Now, if you'd talked to Len you might've been able to keep it secret for a little bit longer. Luckily, this isn't anything that needs to stay on the *hush hush*."

"Definitely not. But I suppose if you've heard about it my explanation can be a little shorter. You know what we're signed up for?"

"I assume Cameron was going to do cleanup for the lot. Tractor work and things like that, and then you and he were going to work on landscaping." Clay continued after she nodded in confirmation. "I'm good with all of that. But I don't know what's involved with the fundraiser."

"Not much on our part. I thought we had to do a lot more organizing, but it turns out we're the hosts for the evening."

Suddenly he looked uncomfortable. "I don't have to talk on a microphone, do I?"

"Don't worry, if there are any announcements to make I can handle that part. It's more that you have to dress up, because there's a dance, and unless one guy commits to going in a suit, no one else will." He pulled a face, and she smiled. "You're as bad as Cameron. Why is it the guys who look the best in suits never want to wear them?"

"Because we know no one is looking at us anyway," he bantered back. "A guy in a suit means a woman in a fancy dress is somewhere close by, and that trumps a guy in a suit any day."

The tease she was going to offer in return was interrupted when his cell phone went off, an annoyingly perky whistle filling the air.

"Damn it, Troy changed my ringtone again." He pulled the phone free from his pocket to check the text message.

Maggie didn't even try to hide her amusement. "Are they sending out a search party for their coffees?"

"Something like that." Clay got to his feet. "I need to run, but how about I come over this week, and we can take a look at what we need to do. Make some plans, that kind of thing."

"I already have a set of master blueprints from Daniel. He said I've got free rein when it comes to designing the layout for walkways and the rest."

Clay nodded as he did up his coat and pulled on his gloves. "You've got the expertise. The committee is lucky to have you."

"And I'm lucky to have *you*," she offered with sincerity. "You're a good friend, Clay. Thank you."

He hesitated for a moment before giving her another of his breath-stealing hugs. Like usual, she felt cared for and guarded as he held her, and like usual, it seemed far too short a time before he set her free and headed out. His phone went off in another round of whistling before the door closed behind him, and the last thing she heard was him cursing his brother, zero heat in the threats to skin him alive.

She laughed and went back to her tasks, not quite sure how to label the emotions roller-coasting through her. It had to have something to do with how right honouring Cameron's memory alongside his good friend was. For the first time in a long time she felt a flutter of excitement. Something to look forward to.

And if there was a tremble of something else there, she wasn't ready to think about it any harder.

CHAPTER 6

What with one thing and another, Maggie managed to convince Clay it was her turn to come over to his place. She stepped into his living room and glanced around with approval. The few times she'd come over with Cameron the place had always struck her as surprisingly homey for a single guy.

"You got a new couch."

"Old couch. I did a trade with Anna and Mitch because mine was a foldout, and they needed it to set up a guest-room-slash-office deal."

"So this was Anna's?" Maggie slipped out of her boots and made her way to the center of the comfortable living room. She dropped her file folder on the coffee table before settling on the brightly patterned couch. "It doesn't really look like Mitch's style." *Come to think of it.* "It doesn't really look like your style, either."

He chuckled as he joined her, sitting in the oversized chair beside her. "Yeah, paisley is so last year, but it's a couch, and it's comfy. I'm not too worried about the mismatching patterns."

They chatted for a while before she felt bad about taking up too much of his evening. She patted the folder. "It's all here. At least the preliminary drawings."

"Great. Let's see what you've got."

He leaned forward, reaching for the file when his phone rang. A solid driving beat plus a flurry of words that included "sexy" then some filthy swearwords.

She'd never seen Clay move so fast. He fumbled for the screen, shutting off the dirty ringtone as soon as possible.

"Let me guess. Troy?"

He rolled his eyes as he stabbed violently at the phone. "I'm surprised that boy has lived as long as he has. He's always one step over the line."

Maggie bit her lip to stop from laughing as Clay made a face. "What's wrong?"

"The bastard changed my password. I can't adjust the ringtone until I choke the new access code out of him." He laid the phone on the chair arm with a heavy sigh. "I'd turn it off completely, but Katy is supposed to text me to arrange babysitting for tomorrow."

"It's not a problem," she assured him.

Only as they looked over the ground blueprints and discussed how to deal with the existing water lines and underground electrical, his phone blared on a regular basis. Clay glanced at each one before hurriedly shutting them down and getting back to their task.

Maggie couldn't remember getting this many calls and texts in one evening her entire life. "You're Mr. Popularity."

When he didn't answer, Maggie glanced up, surprised to find his cheeks had bloomed to red.

"It's nothing. Just my pain-in-the-butt brothers." He hesitated then confessed uneasily, "Their idea of a joke. They signed me up for a dating service and won't tell me the passwords to shut the thing down. I'm getting text messages from women who want to meet me."

Well. That was about the last possible thing she'd expected. "Why on earth would you need a dating service?"

His phone went off. If anything he seemed to turn redder, and Maggie shuffled the papers in front of her to give herself something to do as he dealt with the text. She'd never imagined Clay would be so shy about the fact ladies liked him. A terrible idea popped into her head, one far too tempting to ignore.

"Hey, I know." She offered him a brilliant smile. "There are a few single ladies working at the school. If you need an introduction to any of them—"

"No." The word burst out of him as if jet propelled. He laid the phone on the table between them. "No, *thanks*, I'm okay." She snickered, and this time he shook a finger in her face. "You're as nasty as the rest of them."

"I couldn't resist." She gave up teasing and turned back to the project.

His phone rang, the vibration mode making it bounce across the smooth table and straight over the edge in front of her. She caught it before it could hit the ground, her thumb landing on the screen and accidentally opening the message.

A selfie of a pair of breasts barely covered by a teeny black bra flashed in her face.

"Oh my—"

Her first impulse to toss the phone at Clay was stolen away by sheer shock. It had to be a mistake—she was imagining it. She lifted the phone higher and took a more thorough look.

Nope, she'd been right the first time. "There are boobs on your phone. Anyone I know?"

It was an honest question.

Clay snatched the phone from her fingers, his eyes widening as he glanced at the screen.

"For fucks sake..." He powered it off and tossed it across the room into the other easy chair, growling in frustration. "One of my potential dates wanted to show me her assets."

"She's...well stocked."

He missed the joke, serious concern filling his expression. "I'm sorry you saw that. Hell, I'm sorry *I* saw that."

Maggie quivered with held-back glee. "If you need to work on your portfolio tonight, we can discuss the designs another time."

He gave her a dirty look and that was it. Laughter burst free. It was just he looked so guilty and yet contrite, like a little boy caught with his fingers in the cookie jar. It wasn't her place to judge if he wanted to look at ladies' boobs. Heck, she'd think it was odd if he didn't.

The edges of his mouth twitched until he was smiling as well. "I'm glad you find this entertaining."

"Dating has changed a lot in the eight years Cameron and I were together." The reminder he was gone cut like always, but today, with laughter spilling through her, the pain wasn't as sharp.

Clay leaned back in his chair, dragging a hand through his hair and leaving it a wild mess. "In some ways it hasn't. I mean, it's always been about making yourself attractive to other people. Seeing what you have in common."

"Naked pictures. Yeah, I can see how that proves you have lots in common."

He gestured toward the phone. "That one was pretty tame. You should see some of the stuff people send."

Okay, teasing him might be wrong, but he seemed to think she was some kind of raw innocent. Cameron would have poked him so hard. Maggie pretended to be shocked. "To a total stranger?"

"Yup."

Maggie laid a hand over her chest and gasped like a blue-haired grannie. "Oh God, really? Men too?"

"It happens. *I* don't send out pictures of my junk, I mean—oh, *fuck*."

God, he was adorable, flushing like this was the first discussion he'd ever had regarding sex when she knew *that* wasn't true. She'd overheard him and Cameron plenty of times, and both of them had been plenty frank in their discussions.

It was no use. She gave up and laughed until she had her hands curled around her stomach, gasping for air. Every time she'd nearly gotten herself under control, she'd catch another glimpse of his face, and that would set her off again.

Clay watched with resignation, shaking his head as it finally sank in she'd been pulling his leg.

By the time she'd settled down, he'd grabbed them both drinks and put a plate of snacks on the table in front of her. "Now that the first part of the evening's entertainment is over, we can get back to work."

Happiness bubbled inside her. It felt good to laugh until her stomach ached and her cheeks were warm. She laid her hand on top of his knee and gave it a light squeeze. "You're a good guy, Clay."

"Yeah, I am. Along with a touch gullible..." He shrugged good-naturedly. "Just wait until you set up a profile with a dating service. Then we can compare horror stories."

That she couldn't imagine. "When I start dating again it will not involve naked selfies."

Just saying the words "dating again" made her wonder. She missed Cameron so much, and yet...

There was still laughter in the world. Still love. Maybe even for her.

It was something she'd have to think about more, but not now. Now she had another task. A task that would make a better future for some deserving people, and she was glad to have a good friend at her side as they worked on it.

Clay's expression had gone slightly bemused. "What? What's that look for?"

"Just happy to be here," she confessed. "Ready to get to work, or are you expecting more calls?"

"Very funny."

She chuckled softly as they bent over the blueprints and made plans.

SHE GAVE him another dirty look, and it was so damn cute. "It's a waste of time for you to put on your boots and coat. I do know where I parked," Maggie complained.

"Never said you didn't." Clay let her hang onto his arm as he guided her down the snow-covered front sidewalk. "Good manners aren't a waste of time."

"You're so old fashioned," she teased.

He held the car door for her as she got in. "About some things, yeah. I suppose I am."

Clay stood on the sidewalk after she waved goodbye, waiting until the taillights of her car vanished around the corner.

The urge to sweep in and care for her wasn't going away. The attraction he felt kept growing, and it wasn't just sexual. He'd enjoyed her company before, but he'd been a closer friend with Cameron, especially after Gage's life had gotten busier with Katy and Tanner.

There was definitely a connection between them—him and Maggie. The ease with which she'd laughed made him feel good. Made him want to put that happy expression in her eyes every day, and every moment.

But when? When would it be safe to move?

He'd blundered during a relationship before. Once he'd assumed someone wanted him when they didn't, and that misstep haunted him to this day. Not because he'd been rejected, but because he'd frightened the woman. Seeing her recoil and respond in fear had been enough to scare him off *ever* making assumptions.

Hurting another person had broken something inside him, and he'd sworn he'd never do it again.

Back in the house the contrast between the icy-cold winter evening and the warmth struck like a wall. Hell, it had been hot when Maggie was there, his entire body sensitized by her closeness.

He returned to the living room and tidied up, grabbing his phone off the chair where he'd tossed it. He reluctantly worked through the texts, deleting until he got to the only one he needed—the one from Katy with the time to come and look after Tanner so she and Gage could go out on a date.

As he clicked past some very racy tweets from potential dates, his frustration peaked. Tracking down Troy and sitting on him until both the phone and the damn dating site were fixed moved to the top of his list.

He wandered into his bedroom, stripped his shirt over his head and kicked off his jeans. Tomorrow he'd deal with all the things that had been wrong about tonight, but as he stepped into the shower and turned on the water, his thoughts dwelled on Maggie and where their relationship might go in the future.

He soaped up his hands and ran them over his torso, washing slowly as he considered. Spending the evening with her had fueled the desire for more. And her comment about dating?

While he was glad she didn't plan to mourn forever, her simple words gave him both a rush of hope and kicked his protective instincts into overdrive.

Maggie dating—seeing her dressed up and out on the town for a good time with some other guy—the idea *infuriated* him.

Like *hell* would she ever sign up for a dating service. He might've been the one to suggest it, but his joking words were to cover up what he really wanted to say. What he wanted to offer her, when she was ready.

The sad part was once she was ready, some people in Rocky would judge her. Even if she wore sackcloth for the next ten years, there would be those who assumed her moving on meant things must not have been good between her and Cameron, and Clay knew that was the farthest thing from the truth.

Listening to her laugh had made something inside him come alive in a way he hadn't felt in years. He wanted to savour those moments between them then take the next step. To be allowed to cradle her in his arms. To cup her cheek as she smiled. To lean over and press a kiss to her laughing lips.

Or stroke his hands down her body until he turned her smile to one that was softer, filled with the pleasure he would give her. The pleasures she would give him—

And he was standing in the shower with his fist wrapped around his cock, stroking himself to the thought of her. He was such a fucking bastard.

Didn't mean he was going to stop.

Not when he closed his eyes and could picture her. Soft and happy like she'd been after teasing him. A bright light shining in her eyes as she shared the evening with him. Her lips parted, her body relaxed.

He worked himself harder, running his fingers over the sweet spot on the bottom of his shaft every upstroke. His hand slicked easily over his rock-solid length, between the soap and the water and the fantasy of Maggie sliding her fingers around his dick and taking over. Slipping her tongue along his shaft, teasing him sweetly before wrapping her lips around the head and sucking.

Her big green eyes staring at him full of trust. Full of other emotions—lust and need and fire. Fuck it, he wanted to see her lose control. To be so focused on the pleasure whipping through her body that she turned to him and let him care for her in the most intimate of ways.

The tingling at the base of his spine warned him he was close. His balls drew up, his breathing rapid. He leaned an elbow on the wall of the shower as he stroked faster and imagined her under him. Thrusting into her as she wrapped her arms and legs around him. She'd clutch him tight, her lips open in pleasure, finger nails digging into his back, heels to his butt—

His cock jerked in his hand, seed spurting out in tight, sharp pulses. The warm water cascaded over his shoulders as he worked the last rocking beats of his climax, his breathing ragged, a rush of blood going to his head.

Holy *shit*.

Clay pressed both hands to the shower wall and leaned over as he fought to catch his breath. The water washed away the signs of his recent entertainment, but they couldn't wash away the visions playing out in his head. Things too good to be ignored.

It was a fine line to walk. For now he had to keep pretending. For now he had to keep what he felt a secret from everyone, including Maggie. He wanted to be her friend, but he wanted to be so much more. She wasn't ready, but when she was, no matter how long it took...

He would be there.

CHAPTER 7

Days passed in a blur. Clay kept to his usual routines, spending time with his family and helping Maggie. Planning for the landscaping work they needed to do in the spring gave him the perfect excuse to drop in on a regular basis.

Sometimes they'd discuss the upcoming work. Sometimes she'd talk about what was happening at school, or listen with laughter in her eyes as he'd share about his day at the garage with his brothers.

Slowly she seemed to be waking up, like an echo of spring creeping in on the foothills. One moment the cold clung tightly, the next, dazzling sunshine worked to melt the lingering piles of snow. Clay longed to move forward even as he held himself back.

But today they were gathering for a far more festive reason—Gage and Katy were about to tie the knot.

The late-March day started with cloud-covered sky, but by noon the snow that had threatened moved on. The hustle and bustle around the repair shop had been redirected into tuxedos and formalwear. There were party plans for after the ceremony, and a good old-fashioned dance planned to warm the night.

No way would Maggie miss it, and Clay had every intention of being by her side as much as possible.

"Why the hell do we have to wear monkey suits when *you're* the one getting married?" Troy complained.

Gage didn't answer. He bounced on the balls of his feet in front of the mirror in Clay's bedroom, adjusting his tie for the third time, a goofy grin on his face as he got ready.

"Monkeys, clowns, take your pick," Mitch drawled, the flame-red tattoos on the backs of his hands peeking out as he adjusted the cufflinks on a pristine white dress shirt. "You're part of the three-ring-circus that is a wedding. Stupid invention."

"Says the man who has been engaged for nearly nine months," Len taunted.

Mitch shrugged. "We're working around her schedule. There's some fancy RCMP ritual we can do if we wait until this coming summer. Seems like a lot of fuss to me, but if it makes Anna happy, I can put up with a little bullshit."

"Len's got the right idea," their youngest brother commented, leaning over Gage's shoulder to check in the mirror as he struggled with his tie. "He and Janey just moved in together. I don't see why people do anything else."

"It doesn't matter what *you* think." Gage rotated on the spot and worked on fixing Troy's tie. "It's what the girls want that matters, and if Katy wants me to dress up to make things official, I have zero problem indulging her."

"Pussy whipped," Troy muttered.

"Just like you wish you were," Mitch said with a grin, slapping his brother on the back as they moved into the living room.

They were only moments away from the trip to the hall where the ceremony would take place. Clay was torn between staying with his brothers and best friend, and running ahead to make sure that everything was progressing properly.

Maybe finding Maggie and latching on to her.

But his father was already there taking care of the final details, and the venue had been double-checked. Katy's friends were all over the rest of the organizing that needed to take place.

This was where he was supposed to be, no matter how much he longed to get moving. To take the next step, especially in terms of tracking down Maggie—

—and damn his brain for refusing to lay off thinking about her every other second.

"Five minutes," Troy announced.

Clay and Mitch exchanged glances before closing the gap on Gage.

His best friend glanced up from where he was nervously playing with the ring box. "Why're you looking at me like that?"

Mitch grabbed the box out of Gage's fingers and handed it to Clay. "In the time-honoured tradition of brothers everywhere, this is your final warning. If you *ever* do anything to break Katy's heart, we'll kill you."

Gage's grin just got wider. "What? You're not going to punch me in the face again?"

"You need to look pretty in the wedding pictures. You get a pass for now."

The bridegroom raised a brow. "Your sister and I have been together for more than a year. We have a nine-month-old son, and you've seen how easily she wraps me around her little finger. You *really* think you need to warn me to take care of her?"

A ripple of laughter stole over them before Clay laid a hand on his best friend's shoulder. "We've been through a lot together since we were fifteen. You've been my best friend through some of the roughest times in my life, and you're already like a brother to me."

Gage nodded slowly, waiting...

"But Katy's our sister. Hurt her, and we'll skin you alive."

His lips twisted into a cocky smile. "Good thing I don't plan on doing anything to make her unhappy. *Ever.*"

Good-natured teasing continued all the way to the reception hall. There was a rush of last-minute things to deal with before Clay found himself standing at the front of the room next to Gage, the Justice of the Peace at their side.

Katy and her friends had decorated the hall the night before. Simple folding chairs were lined up in rows, twisted streamers looping along the edge to create a path to the front of the hall. Instead of flowers, they'd filled silver feed-buckets with branches from willow trees that had been forced into budding early. Above the white pussy willows were cutout snowflakes hung on fishing line, dozens of them tacked to the ceiling until the room looked as if they were in the midst of a storm where the snow never hit the ground.

Background music played softly. Clay looked through the audience gathering as Len and Troy seated the guests as they arrived.

"The longest five minutes of my entire life," Gage whispered under his breath.

"Nah. Longest five minutes will be when Katy hesitates before saying *I do*, and you wonder if she's about to freak out and run, or not."

The colour drained from Gage's face. "She wouldn't."

God. Clay hurried to reassure him, but couldn't hide his grin. "No, she wouldn't. For some reason she's crazy about you, so relax."

Gage gave him a dirty look then focused on the back of the room, stiffening then releasing a tormented sigh as the doors swung open another time without it being Katy and the start of the ceremony.

Maggie arrived. Len walked her down the aisle and seated her right where Clay had a direct line of vision to her face.

He didn't even pretend not to stare.

Her long brown hair had been cut to shoulder length, reddish-gold flashes reflecting the light as she turned to greet her neighbors. She wore a pale-green sweater that looked soft to the touch, and Clay wanted to leave his post immediately to test his theory.

Only the sound of people rising to their feet and processional music beginning to play kept him in place. But his focus stayed on her, taking in every detail, every line—soaking her in.

She looked fragile, but more rested than she'd been lately. Her green eyes were highlighted by the colour of her top. She glanced forward, smiling as she spotted Gage, the man constantly shifting his weight as he waited for Katy to appear.

Then her eyes met Clay's.

He wanted to think there was a connection. That she somehow reacted to him, but suddenly all attention turned to the wedding party breaching the back doors, and the moment slipped away.

Janey came first, holding a bright-eyed teeny-tuxedo clad nine-month-old Tanner in her arms as she paced directly in front of her friend. Katy stepped slowly down the aisle, fingers clasped around their father's arm. Keith's expression was dead serious, as if he was holding back tears.

As soon as Janey reached the front of the room, Tanner thrust out his arms to Gage, loudly demanding a transfer. The entire group of friends gathered to witness the wedding chuckled as Gage took his son from Janey with a grin.

"No reason why he can't be a part of this."

He held Tanner with an experienced air as Katy joined him, and they faced the JP to begin the ceremony.

The words rolled over them. Clay listened, but he was more interested in the deep satisfaction spinning in his gut as his family surrounded the couple. His father nodded in approval as Katy and Gage exchanged vows, making promises to be there for each other—in the good times, in the bad. As the ceremony continued, Clay let his gaze drift to take in the rest of those he cared for. Len and Janey stood next to Anna Coleman who was beaming suspiciously hard as she held Mitch's hand. Troy fidgeted a little, his gaze darting to the back of the room, but he too was smiling.

Maggie's gaze remained fixed on the bride and groom, and Clay gave himself one last moment to linger on her before refocusing his attention as well.

"I'll always be yours, and you'll always be mine." Gage adjusted his son then slipped the ring on Katy's finger. He offered Tanner the empty box, and he caught hold with two hands, instantly lifting it to his mouth to chew on it.

Katy's eyes sparkled.

"Going forward," Gage promised, "the only thing that'll ever change is I'm going to love you more every single day."

The officiate said a few more words, and then there was kissing accompanied by applause from the audience.

The JP cleared his throat. "Before any of you leave, we need just a moment."

Clay stiffened. This wasn't on the agenda.

Katy and Gage whispered together, both of them grinning widely as they stood in the middle of the platform, looking out at their friends as Tanner played happily in Gage's arms.

"Have a seat. We'll be with you in a minute," Katy announced, waving a hand.

Meanwhile, Anna Thompson had tugged Mitch to one side. Mitch looked worried as hell. He spoke softly, but loud enough the family at the front overheard.

"What's wrong?" he demanded.

"Nothing." She glanced at the family then leaned closer to Mitch. "Would you like to get married today?" she asked.

A murmur of voices had risen over the entire reception hall as people waited to find out what was happening, but at the front of the room the echoing silence was broken only by Tanner's childish laugh.

Mitch's mouth opened and shut a couple times, but no words came out.

"Planning our wedding has become a madhouse," Anna confessed, "so I asked Katy and Gage if they'd be okay with us crashing their party, and they said sure."

Mitch pulled it together, glancing into the hall. "Is that why your family is here?"

Anna nodded. "They don't know specifics, though, so it's your call. Instead of wasting more time planning, we can make it short, sweet, and to the point. You ready to do this thing?"

He flashed a smile at Anna that was cocky, dangerous, and one hundred percent possessive. "Hell, yeah. Good with me."

A buzz had built through the room as rumours flew. Mitch looked a little shell-shocked but his grin was real as he turned to his family. "You guys ready to do this all over again?"

Katy slipped over to offer him a kiss on the cheek before straightening his collar and tie. "I'm glad we can share this day with you. You should check if your father-in-law wants to give his daughter way."

"Shit, good idea," Mitch muttered. He glanced at Anna. "Hell, why not the whole family?"

Delight shone on her face.

"Are we good to go?" the Justice of the Peace asked. "I already have your paperwork in place. Once you're organized, we'll get started."

Mitch turned to the room and cleared his throat.

"Big favour to ask. Stick around for a little longer." He faced Anna's family who sat to one side of the room. "Anna and I are getting married. You want to come up here and be our witnesses?"

Controlled bedlam ensued.

There were so many people standing up that, in the end, everyone grabbed their chairs and rearranged the room. Friends settled in one corner while the Thompson and Coleman clans gathered in the other, and then everyone listened as Mitch and Anna off-the-cuff made up their vows.

It was no accident Clay ended up standing next to Maggie who was grinning just as hard as the rest of the witnesses. She linked her fingers around his arm and squeezed tightly.

Clay held his breath, not wanting to spook her away.

Mitch caught both Anna's hands in his as if he needed

to keep her from bolting. He shook his head, his expression a mix of disbelief and sheer utter happiness. "It's going to take a million fucking years to figure you out, Anna Coleman, and I'm going to have a blast every minute, of every fucking day."

Her smile widened, but she didn't say anything.

"I swear I'll be there for you, no matter where we live, or what life hands us. It's you and me, babe, rock-fucking solid. And if I ever get stupid, you just handcuff me to some immovable object until my brain comes back online."

The JP cleared his throat, but didn't interrupt.

"I can't fucking believe that you love me, but I'm glad. So damn glad. And you're never going to regret this, I swear."

The longer Mitch went on, the more Anna's lips twitched until she gave up, her small snickers blooming into full-out laughter. "Only you, Mitch Thompson. Only you."

Mitch raised a brow. "Are those your vows? Because, fuck, that's all I need to hear. That's all I'm *ever* going to need."

Joy bubbled inside Maggie, for the first time in a long time, as she witnessed the surprise double wedding. The final vows said, the JP turned to the gathering.

"Ladies and gentlemen, I'm proud to present your newlyweds: Gage and Katy Jenick, *and* Mitch and Anna Thompson."

Maggie released her grip on Clay's arm to add her applause to those around her. It felt as if the room was filled with sparkling air and sunshine, but it wasn't just the beams of light coming in the windows. There was so much love expressed in the faces around her...

Suddenly she couldn't breathe. While everyone was cheering and stepping forward to offer congratulations, Maggie slipped away, moving through the crowd as quickly as she could toward the back rooms.

At the end of the hall, she found an unlocked door. She snuck in and discovered a nursery with toys in neat boxes along one wall, and rocking chairs tucked behind a small freestanding wall. She headed toward the window, looking for something to concentrate on other than the flood of emotion that had rushed in far too quickly.

Sorrow was the wrong word. That was there as always, but now some other emotion was squeezing her heart. And when understanding hit, the truth shocked her.

As happy as she was for Katy and the others, she was *jealous*.

Maggie leaned her hands on the top of the small bookcase and stared out the window at the piles of snow covering the lawn of the community hall. She picked up the bundle of confusion inside her and methodically pulled apart.

It wasn't even that they were a couple, and she no longer had Cameron. That pain was easing, as unbelievable as it seemed. She missed him like hell, but he wasn't coming back. She knew that, accepted it, but there were other parts of having a relationship she missed so much. Having someone always there to smile with, someone to share her life with.

She was straight-up envious of the new couples' joy, and that was no one's fault. Or maybe...

No. It was no one's fault, *period*. But it was time for change. Time for her to allow happiness into her life again.

Laughter spilled down the hall. She retreated to the far corner of the room, hoping no one would interrupt her while she worked this out.

Her wish didn't work. The door swung open and someone came in. Someone swore—a familiar voice—the word muttered softly in the room behind her.

Footsteps rang across the floor and Maggie retreated farther, tucked behind the barrier. She wasn't sure why she was hiding, but even as she decided to come forward a low, masculine voice rumbled, and she froze on the spot, wondering why Clay was there.

"You're a fucking tease, Nicole."

"Maybe you just don't know how to solve the puzzle that is me," a soft, feminine voice taunted back.

Something crashed to the floor followed by heavy breathing. Maggie's heart rate accelerated. There was no way she could step out, but she was completely confused.

What was Clay doing?

"Oh, hell *yes*," Nicole whispered. "Do it. Right now."

"You're not calling the shots anymore," he said. "Put your hands against the wall and keep them there."

Maggie couldn't stand it any longer. She leaned forward and peered through the miniscule gap in the fabric barriers separating her from the rest of the room.

It wasn't Clay, it was *Troy*, and she would spend more time dwelling on the similarities in their voices later, but she was too busy keeping silent as he leaned against Nicole, pressing her to the wall with his body as he took her lips in a hungry kiss.

Nicole lifted her hands to his shoulders, and he growled at her, catching her wrists in one hand then pressing them over her head. The position stretched her, arching her into him as he caught her chin with his other hand.

"Don't move your hands," he commanded.

From where Maggie stood, only a thin slice of Nicole's face was visible, and the other woman's eyes widened, cheeks flushing as she obeyed and caught hold of the only thing above her head—the end of the curtain rod.

This time Troy hummed in approval. "There we go. If you keep them there, I'll give you a present."

Nicole licked her lips. "Is it a nice present?"

"One of the very best," Troy promised.

Then he kissed his way down her body, hands sliding along her waist. As he knelt before her, Nicole tilted her face toward him, her breathing unsteady.

Maggie covered her mouth with a hand. She should look away. She should let them know she was there, no matter how embarrassing that would be.

But what she *should* do, and what she *wanted* to do were polar extremes at that moment. She couldn't tear eyes away as Troy set Nicole squirming, his hands and lips bringing forth the most amazing sounds from her lips.

And when he knelt in front of her, bunching up her skirt to press a kiss over her mound, Nicole's eager anticipation was clear. Arms stretched overhead, she waited until he'd pulled down her panties and pantyhose then stepped her legs apart. "Please…"

Troy traced a finger down her belly, slowly sliding over her sex. "So pretty. You're so pretty down here."

"Don't you dare tease me," Nicole whispered. "We have to be back out for the reception in just a few minutes. "

"You're not calling the shots," Troy reminded her.

But when she would've protested, he leaned forward and put his mouth to her, tongue flicking against the apex of her sex. Nicole moaned in approval, widening her stance and pressing her hips forward.

Troy worked quickly, his tongue and fingers teasing over Nicole's body. Maggie's temperature rose as well, a feeling of longing competing with other unsatisfied urges.

Damn it. She twisted away, facing the wall, no longer spying. But every sound, every moan, every *thing* played out in her imagination as if she'd been watching on a high-definition screen.

It seemed only seconds later Nicole uttered his name, followed immediately by another throaty cry of pleasure. Troy echoed the sound, and a curious thumping noise began.

Oh *God*. Maggie clenched her fists together and stared at the wall in front of her, pulling in her strength. Refusing to look even though it was very clear exactly what was taking place in the room behind her.

"So fucking good," Troy gasped. "So. Fucking. Good."

Each of his final words was punctuated with a solid bang, and Nicole spoke, just above a whisper but as loud as a shout in Maggie's ears. Troy joined her then all but their heavy breathing faded. Low, murmured laughter followed as they got themselves together. Vanishing from the room as if they'd never been there.

Only from the pounding in her heart and the ache centered low in Maggie's belly, there was no doubt that the couple had impacted her world.

Was she jealous of joy?

She was definitely jealous of *pleasure*.

It was time. It was time for her to begin to live.

Maggie leaned her shoulders against the bookcase and waited for *her* breathing to return to normal, but nothing would ever be the same.

It might take courage to deal with this new reality, but

the truth was, in a way she felt she'd been preparing for this moment for a long time.

She wanted passion in her life? She didn't have to look far to know *who* she wanted to turn to for help.

Not today. Not this moment, but soon. Very soon.

If he was interested—

CHAPTER 8

April trundled in slowly. Winter clung tightly to the foothills with a new dump of snow followed by a cold snap. Clay worked in the shop and teased Gage and Mitch, both of whom wandered around as if they were giddy-drunk half the time. Mitch especially—he and Anna had gotten away for a week to Hawaii as a wedding gift from the Coleman clan, and he hadn't stopped grinning since he got back.

Seeing his rebel of a brother absolutely beaming with happiness gave Clay a great deal of satisfaction, and a twinge or two of jealousy.

He watched over Maggie from afar damn near every day, and he was over at her place a few times a week, but lately she'd seemed distracted, even twitchy in his presence. It was hard not to take her reactions personally, even though it had to be because she was going through a tough time. She refused to say anything, though, and he didn't want to make things worse by poking where he wasn't wanted.

All his protective instincts were at war. Charge in or hold back and keep silently looking out for her?

The evening of the gala rolled around, and he had no answer other than waiting to see what came next.

He dressed with moderate enthusiasm. Even if he had to wear a suit and tie, and even if he was going to be in pain all night, he still got to be with her and hold her while they danced...

At this point he'd take any damn crumb he could.

She opened the door in answer to his knock, and Clay nearly swallowed his tongue. "Holy *shit.*"

Maggie pirouetted in front of him. "You like? Katy helped pick it out."

Didn't matter who had helped, it was the end result that had him in instant severe lust. Deep green fabric clung to every curve of her body, wrapping around her breasts and hips before coming to a stop mid-thigh. The material drew him forward, and the desire to touch shot skyward.

Hell, he wanted to stroke his hand over her shoulders, down her waist. Pull her against him until there wasn't a lick of air between them. And after they'd spent the evening dancing with every inch of them rubbing together, he'd take her home, strip her out of the dress and put them back into that same position until the sun came up.

That was what raced through Clay's mind.

What managed to escape his lips was a casual, "You look great."

She smiled, pleasure trailing across her face at his faint praise. "I'm ready to go," she said, slipping on her coat before he could offer to help, his brain numb from fighting to control his body's reaction.

Helping her into his truck only compounded his problems as he was confronted with the long line of her smooth thighs, her dress riding up. She tugged the edge downward, but the meager inch it moved was no help.

Maggie laid a hand on his arm. "Wait, I forgot the prize bags."

She wiggled toward the door, exposing more of her thighs all over. *God almighty.* Clay jerked up a hand to stop her. "I'll get them."

The time in the cold night air should have helped him regain control, but it wasn't long enough to completely cool him off. It only took a couple of minutes before he returned to the driver side of the truck, intending to put the bags between them.

Instead, Maggie took them from his hands and placed them on the passenger seat. "I thought you were going to open the side door, so I'm already buckled in the middle."

The shot of adrenaline that raced through him was wrong in so many ways. Clay got behind the wheel and deliberately focused on every task one by one. Seatbelt. Start the engine. Vehicle in gear. Back out of the driveway.

It was no use. Every action was instinctive which gave him plenty of time to daydream about *accidentally* moving his hand until it rested on the curve of her thigh—

Dammit. He silently kicked his own ass. He'd lasted until now; he would wait however long he had to. It was only April, for fuck's sake. That said, he needed to control himself far better than this, or he would freak her out.

Clay cleared his throat. "We'll be at the restaurant in a few minutes."

She shivered, leaning toward him. "I didn't realize how much the temperature had dropped. I should've worn a warmer coat."

He was already moving before he realized he was asking for trouble. There was no alternative—he draped his arm around her shoulders and pulled her close. Her warm, feminine scent filled his head, and his entire body tightened into one mass of need.

The fucking evening was going to fucking drive him to the fucking madhouse.

She sat quietly, and he wondered if he'd let slip some of the dirty thoughts rolling through his brain. But when she spoke it was on a different topic altogether.

"I just realized something. I don't think I've danced with you. Or at least, not since high school Phys Ed."

He knew they hadn't. If they had, the memory would've been etched into his brain and driven his anticipation higher. "Don't worry, we'll be fine."

Her hand rested lightly on his leg, and he pinned his lips together to keep from growling in frustration. A few inches to the left and she'd get an unwelcome surprise, his cock pressed hard to the front of his dress pants.

"I'm not worried about dancing." A small laugh escaped her, and fuck it all, if she didn't sound slightly nervous. "You did turn off your phone, though, didn't you? Because I don't think I can handle being interrupted by your harem while we're on the dance floor."

Damn dating service. Clay groaned. "Stop teasing about that. You know how long it took for me to get the access codes out of Troy."

"You were one second away from wringing his neck." She squeezed his leg and set off another round of fireworks along his nervous system. "Next time, you let me talk to him. *I'll* intimidate him. Make him see the error of his ways."

"Ha, there'd better not be a next time." He pulled into the parking lot and smiled at the thought of Maggie lecturing his little brother. "Hell, you're right, there'll be another time. This is *Troy* we're talking about."

"He's not that bad. I can handle him."

Clay snickered as he found a spot in the nearly empty restaurant parking lot. "You go right ahead. Make sure you let me know when you plan to start so I can watch."

"You don't think I'd do it," Maggie said, her eyes sparkling.

"Don't know why you would."

She didn't say anything but her expression grew more determined, and Clay wondered what on earth was going on. Then he was distracted as some of the committee met them at the door and took the bags from their hands.

Allison Coleman stepped forward as the others retreated. "Thanks for picking Parker's Timberline Grill for the event. If you need anything, let me know. I'll be around all night to troubleshoot."

"Do you know if Daniel is here already?" Clay asked.

Allison gestured toward the back of the restaurant where there was a large banquet room. "He and Beth are checking everything's in place. The rest of your committee headed back to their tables in the restaurant to wait for the guests to arrive." She smiled. "I opened the bar already, so they're happy."

Clay helped Maggie out of her coat then ended up with her hands wrapped around his arm as they made their way down the narrow hallway to where the second half of the party would take place.

He'd gotten control of his body during the short time from the truck to the restaurant. He needed to keep it that way for the rest of the night, especially with the eagle-eyed crew that would be around for the fundraiser—he didn't need one of them getting suspicious that he had the hots for Maggie.

One of the downfalls of a small town. *Someone* would

take it upon themselves to let her know, probably along with an earful about how terribly disgusting and callous it was for him to make a move so soon.

The banquet hall was decorated far better than any school gymnasium he remembered, although the dances he'd attended had come to an abrupt halt after his mom died.

"You guys did an amazing job finishing up after I left yesterday. It looks gorgeous." Maggie rotated slowly, admiration on her face as she took in the festive surroundings.

Beth Coleman gave a little curtsey, her dark hair arranged in cascading curls that bounced as she moved. "Most of that is because of Katy and Janey. The two of them put together the whole design."

Her husband stepped behind her. Daniel settled an arm around Beth possessively. "A good design helps, but you need to take a compliment when you're given one, sweetheart. You ladies did a great job." He dropped a kiss against her temple then spotted Clay, reaching a hand in greeting.

"Good to see you."

"Me too." Daniel grinned. "And that's not just a line. I'm *damn* glad to see you. Now that you're here, I get to sit in the background and dance with my wife while you do the heavy lifting with Maggie."

"Now who's not taking credit for everything he's done," Beth whispered loudly, resting her hand against his chest as she smiled up at him.

Clay barely kept from shouting in surprise as Maggie slipped her hand into his. "It's been a lot of fun working with both of you. I'm glad we could be part of the event."

Beth's eyes sparkled. "I hope you say that at the end of the evening."

Maggie tugged on his fingers. "We'd better get back to the door to start our *heavy lifting*."

He dipped his head in farewell then followed along obediently, hoping she didn't notice his hand was getting sweaty just from holding hers. *God*. He was a teenager all over again, with his heart pounding from imagining something that was definitely not happening.

There were an awful lot of *we* and *our* falling from Maggie's lips, but...he was sure she didn't mean anything by it.

She pulled to a stop in the darkness of the hallway just before the front entrance and examined him carefully. The next thing he knew she was adjusting his tie and tugging the lapels of his collar into position. Then damn if she didn't lift her hand and run her fingers through his hair to straighten it, nodding with satisfaction when she was done. "There you go. You were a little rumpled."

Sweet Jesus, he wanted to be a whole lot *more* rumpled.

She lifted her face to his expectantly. "What about me?"

He stood in stunned silence for a few seconds. "What about you...*what*?"

She rolled her eyes. "Be my mirror. Do I look okay? Do I need to be straightened out anywhere?"

Goddamn. Faced with a direct order he had no choice but to check her out her from top to bottom, his body tightening with wicked heat. He smoothed a hand from her waist over her hip to remove a small wrinkle left from sitting in the truck.

It was as soft as he'd thought it would be. Her dress. And her *under* the fabric, and he might've forgotten to breathe for a few seconds before he snapped out of his

87

stupor in time to keep from doing something terrible. Something like taking three steps forward, pressing her to the wall and kissing the living daylights out of her.

He lifted his gaze and met her eyes, her lash-fluttering sending another set of confused messages romping through him like runaway horses. He cleared his throat and tried to sound casual. "You look great."

She dipped her chin and took a deep breath. "Then I guess we should go play hosts."

HER HEART WAS STILL BEATING FASTER than normal fifteen minutes later as the guests continued to arrive. She stood beside Clay and offered greetings, directing the partygoers toward their tables in the restaurant.

She had worried for a while that the evening would turn into a "how are you dear" opportunity for the people who hadn't seen her since Cameron's funeral, but so far everyone had been simply focused on an evening out and a good time.

They took her and Clay acting as greeters in stride. Only a couple of inquisitive glances seemed to assess if there was more below the surface.

Oh God, she hoped so...

It had taken all her courage to pour herself into the dress, let alone begin to flirt with Clay. It'd been so long since she'd had to assess whether a new man was interested in her, but from her early attempts it didn't seem as if he was going to run screaming from her presence.

Of course, that was a long way from actually being interested in her—in a relationship. They were already friends. Could it be that much further of a step for them to become more?

She glanced at him, skimming her gaze over his square jaw. Over the solid breadth of his shoulders as he stood beside her and chatted with two of the older members of the community. He seemed to know a little about everyone who had shown up so far, and she was impressed.

"You not only dress up nice, you know how to woo them." She leaned against his side during a break between arrivals, smiling as she whispered so they weren't overheard. "You should run for mayor."

He looked flustered for a moment before cracking a smile. "Just good business sense."

"You sure you don't want to be in charge of tonight's program? Say the word and I'll give you control of the microphone."

"Hell no." He raised a brow as he twisted toward her, crossing his broad arms in front of his chest. "Don't you go changing the rules on me. People didn't come here to listen to me yatter, and they certainly don't want to look at me when they could look at you."

She smoothed his tie as an excuse to put her hands against his chest again. "Fifty percent of the room would disagree with you," she teased. "But don't worry, you can stay at the table where no one gets to ogle you."

The door opened before he could respond, and she was back beside him, no indication that what she'd wanted to do was slide her hands up until she could join them behind his neck. Then she'd tug him down far enough she could press their lips together.

It was a good thing Clay was doing the small talk, because she found herself flustered wondering whether he would kiss slow and soft, or hungrily—because right then she had no idea which she would prefer.

She missed kissing and cuddling. She missed dirty talk

and sexual innuendo, but most of all she missed *sex*. That total abandonment of physical control in the moments just before climax—that sensation wasn't something she'd managed to duplicate using her fingers or any toy. She and Cameron had enjoyed each other's company in bed as well as out of it, and when she said she missed him, it was true. She missed *everything* that they'd had together.

Orgasms were wonderful, but they were even more magical when they were shared.

And *that* dirty thought was on her mind instead of trying to remember the name of the owner of the local feed mill.

She pulled it together long enough to send the couple on their way to the right table. As tempting as her plans were for the evening, she really had to keep her mind on more than one thing.

They finally moved toward the dining hall where the restaurant was serving the food family style. Casual appetizers were followed by more formal courses, and in between each, she and Clay chatted with the people at their table. She excused herself and popped up to the podium at intervals, handing out door prizes that had been donated by the local companies, and otherwise keeping the evening moving forward at a steady pace.

It was a simple and enjoyable event, and she was busy enough to be distracted briefly from her other agenda for the night.

Then she turned back toward her table and caught Clay looking at her with an expression that could be only described as hungry. Hope made her stutter as she quickly focused elsewhere, but that brief moment of complete honesty she'd seen was exactly what she needed to continue her plan of attack.

Once dinner was done, everyone moved down the hall into the banquet area. Maggie found herself shaking with anticipation. Like a teen with a crush, all she could think about was the moment Clay would take her in his arms and she'd be allowed to stay there. Breathing in the scent of him, touching in a way she hadn't been allowed to up until now.

"Do you need a break?" he asked as a dark-haired young man fiddled with the sound system, getting the music ready to go. "Joel will have that ready in a minute."

Tables and chairs lined the perimeter of the room leaving a wide-open space in the center. Smiling faces were everywhere as people found places to put their things, but already couples hovered at the edge of the dance floor.

"I'm good to go." She glanced at him. Somewhere between the dinner table and now he'd grown serious. That wasn't the mood she had hoped to inspire. "I forgot to ask you a very important question."

Clay offered his elbow as he led them toward the sound system, walking slower than usual in deference to her high heels. "It's too late to ask if I can dance," he teased.

"P'shaw. I already know you can." Whatever delay had caused problems seemed to be solved as music swelled, filling the room. She turned to face him, looking up into his dark brown eyes as he pulled her into position and placed his hand around her waist. "Which of us is going to lead?"

His solemn expression vanished, and Clay threw back his head and laughed, drawing attention from others in the room who were also taking their first steps. Smiles reflected back at them, along with a few curious expressions, but she didn't care. Maggie was focused on him.

"Why's that so funny?" she asked

Clay was already moving them to the music, their feet stepping in perfect synchronization. "If you're trying to tell me Cam didn't lead when you went dancing, I'm going to call bullshit."

"I never said that," she teased. "I asked what *you* needed. But since it seems to be a moot point, forget I even mentioned it."

She had better things to do, like enjoy the way his hand felt spread against her lower back as he guided her across the dance floor. Their bodies close together as they swayed, her breasts brushing his chest, the heat from his torso more than making up for the thin fabric of her dress.

Those dance classes way back when in high school—she would have totally lost marks for placing her hand in the wrong position. Instead of resting it lightly on his shoulder, she slid her fingers farther up until she touched the hair at the back of his neck.

As they circled the floor, she found her fingertips pressed to his warm neck, moving against him in a way that set her heart pounding yet wasn't about to get them arrested for acting indecent.

Around them the floor was filled with couples, laughing and dancing, focused on their own little worlds. Maggie took a deep breath and let it out slowly, tempted to rest her head against Clay's chest as the tempo of the music slowed.

He adjusted his grip and that's when she heard it. An unsteady breath, his throat moving in a hard swallow. She caught his gaze and scalding heat reflected back. He didn't try to hide or deny it—in that moment there was no doubt that Clay Thompson wanted her for more than a friend.

And...a wave of uncertainty set in. It was fantastic news—*not*.

Because she wasn't sure how to take the next step. She knew what she wanted, oh *God*, she knew what she wanted.

Still, she couldn't help feeling slightly relieved when the DJ announced it was time for a break. She needed some air before she crawled all over him right there in public.

CHAPTER 9

By the time they'd said their goodbyes and headed to the truck, Clay was nearly vibrating.

He didn't know which way was up anymore.

There was no reason for Maggie to take the middle seat in the truck on the way home, but damn if he didn't want her there. Instead of leading her to the passenger side, Clay walked her to the driver door and pulled it open, helping her up the step to the bench seat. If his hands lingered a little longer than they did a few hours ago, he blamed it on the near drunken euphoria rolling through his veins from having spent the entire evening breathing in the sweet scent of her perfume. From holding her in his arms where he'd longed to have her.

Maggie buckled up in the middle, waving goodbye to the last of the fundraiser attendees who smiled before turning away.

Clay concentrated as he put the truck into gear and slowly made his way out of the parking lot. He wasn't sure what was going on—he *wasn't* going to make any assumptions—but what the community would be talking about within the next twenty-four hours was another matter altogether.

He was trying to figure out how to approach his worries when Maggie laid her head on his shoulder, her hands slipping around his arm. "Thank you for being there with me. Thank you for making the evening such a success."

"No bother at all," he said, and he meant every word even as he planned what he would do if anyone dared give her grief for shining so brightly.

There would always be the naysayers and the negative element who could find something to complain about. And damn if he ever wanted to see her happiness disappear again.

They sat in silence until he reached Maggie's house. Her grip on his arm and the warmth of her right there next to him only made the longings that had begun earlier in the evening stronger.

"Come in for a drink?" she asked.

Clay didn't bother to offer any of that "it's late" bullshit. He wanted to come in so bad he could taste it.

Still he held back as he led her to the house. He removed her coat without pressing his lips to that spot on the back of her neck he'd been longing to kiss all night. He managed to keep from catching hold of her hand and jerking her into his arms so he could ravish her lips.

Instead, he followed her into the living room, surprised when she pulled out whiskey tumblers and poured them each two fingers neat of Cameron's favourite whiskey. The bottle he'd given his friend for his birthday back in the fall.

Thirty years old was far too young to die.

Maggie pressed a glass into his hand. Her eyes were moist, but she smiled and raised her drink in the air. "To a brighter future."

He touched his glass to hers with a gentle clink, then they both drank. The golden liquid burned a fiery path down Clay's throat. Warmth spread to his chest and gut as they put the glasses aside.

Nothing between them but a foot of air.

Her eyes were mesmerizing. Her tongue darted over her lips as she licked away the last of the liquor. Her breathing accelerated, her chest moving like seduction under that damn dress that showed off her figure to perfection.

She lifted a hand and laid it over his chest, and there was no way to deny the solid thumping she must've felt against her palm.

"What are we doing?" he whispered. He had to be certain.

"Living."

God. He laid a hand over hers, pinning her in place. With his other hand, he slid his fingers past her cheek, stroking his thumb over her cheekbone. Soft skin under his touch, bright eyes staring into his as her lips opened partway, an invitation he craved to accept. "Are you sure?"

She nuzzled against his palm, her eyes closing as she moved against him. "I want this. I want you."

Any hesitation he might have had washed away in that moment. The sheer utter longing in her tone told him all he needed. He slipped his hand around the back of her neck, fingers nestled into her hair as he cupped her head and tilted it so he could lean forward and brush his lips over hers.

A brief, gentle touch. Just enough to take a first taste.

His entire body had gone hard, every muscle primed as she moved against him like she had on the dance floor. But now he could give in to the cravings he had—and he intended to. One exquisite moment at a time.

Like being given keys to a vintage wine cellar, he didn't want to rush and miss a single moment of the experience.

He spread his fingers on her lower back and brought their bodies even closer as he went for another kiss. This one more intense, asking for more, slipping his tongue against her lips until she opened to him and let him in.

His previous fantasies had nothing on the real thing. As Maggie stirred against him, warm breath mixing with his and womanly curves pressed against his hardness, he was glad. It was a brand-new experience. It was enough to blow his mind.

He moved them backward, tempted to rush ahead, ripping away her dress until she stood naked before him. He wanted to be buried in her so badly.

But no matter how much she said she wanted this, he needed to be sure. He paused when his calves hit the couch, breaking the distance between them so he could look into her eyes and check she was fully on board.

Her lips were swollen from his kisses, wet with moisture. Her pupils were wide, and she stared back, panting heavily.

"God, I could eat you up in one bite," he breathed. He cupped her face in his hands, kissing her in spite of his intentions to slow down.

She jerked open his dress jacket and shoved it from his shoulders. He let go of her so he could toss it aside.

Maggie caught him by surprise and planted a hand on his chest, pushing him onto the couch before lifting the edge of her skirt so she could straddle his thighs and settle in his lap. "Don't mind me. I have this *thing* I've wanted to do for a while. It requires undressing you."

Clay had no objections. "I plan to return the favour."

She loosened his tie, her eyes serious as she worked the

silk from around his neck. She pulled it free then dropped it on top of his jacket. He wasn't sure what to watch—her face as she worked on the buttons of his dress shirt, or his hands as he eased them up her bare thighs under the raised portion of her dress.

"I like your hands on me," she admitted with a purr of pleasure.

"I'm glad. I plan to have them there for a good long time."

He caught her licking her lips, and he skimmed his hands up the outside of her dress, pulling her forward as he stole in for another kiss. His shirt hung open, and the warm swells of her breasts pressed against him through her dress.

It wasn't enough. He wanted bare skin to bare skin, but he didn't want to miss taking one step at a time.

And kissing her—

Fuck, he could do that all night.

Still, he couldn't resist tugging the zipper of her dress down as he seduced her with his lips. The straps on her shoulders opened wider, slipping off as the top slid away.

"Sweet mercy, Maggie."

She leaned back and wiggled her arms free, and he was left with the most beautiful view—she wore nothing but silky skin from the waist up. A smooth expanse of honey-coloured skin, her nipples tight pink buttons.

"I think my heart stopped." Clay eased his hands up the sides of her waist until he was level with her breasts, his thumbs under the soft weight of the curves. He circled his thumbs upward and over the tight peaks, and Maggie arched into his touch, her head falling back as he played.

"That feels so good," she whispered. "Don't stop. More."

The only way he could've stopped was if the house was on fire. And even then it would've been a tough decision.

He alternated between cupping and fondling her, and only when her small gasps and moans forced him past the breaking point, he caught hold of her hips and lifted her. He brought her in line with his mouth then licked from the bottom curve to her nipple before closing his lips around it and sucking.

Maggie speared her fingers through his hair as if locking him in position. She didn't have to worry, he had no intention of going anywhere. Licking and sucking and teasing until she squirmed against him, hips riding forward instinctively as she looked for something to rub against.

"Shh. It's okay, sweetheart. I'll make you feel real good."

She dipped her head, returning his gaze with pure, clear honesty. "I feel amazing."

They had only begun, and holy hell, *this* was what he had longed for. She was perfect. *They* were perfect.

MAGGIE WAS BURNING UP. It wasn't about how long it had been, it was about how Clay made her feel, right here and now.

It seemed as if there were two of him. The kind and caring man who had been her friend when that was what she needed. And this sexy, irresistible man she was taking as a lover—it was because she'd had the one that she could accept the other.

She twisted from his grasp and off the couch so she could tug him to his feet. "Come on."

He followed, his fingers twined with hers as she led him down the hallway. She considered stopping at the guest room, but that wasn't what she wanted. Turning their bedroom into some kind of shrine would have made Cameron laugh his head off. She was smiling as she carried on the final few steps into the large master bedroom.

She whirled on Clay so she could strip away his already unbuttoned dress shirt. "My turn to drive you mad."

He went willingly, obligingly leaning back on the wall where she placed him, although she had the feeling he was humouring her.

"You've been doing that all evening, so why should I expect you to change your game plan?"

Maggie trailed her hand down his chest, her fingers teasing the flat disk of one nipple on the way to his abdomen. "That wasn't *all* intentional."

His muscles flexed under her fingers. "Of course not. You accidentally kept brushing me." He smiled at her, a sparkle in his eyes that showed he was having fun as well as getting turned on. "And you had *no* idea what you were doing to me while we were dancing."

Maggie eased her hand over the length of his erection pressing hard to the front of his dress pants. "No, that part was intentional."

It felt so good to touch him. To hear groans escape his lips as she leaned forward and pressed her lips to his chest.

She took her time, tracing her fingertips over firm abdominal muscles, dragging her thumb under the edge of his belt then along the edge of his Adonis muscle.

She caught hold of his belt and hauled one side free, lifting her lips for a kiss.

His expression changed to one of deep frustration. Clay caught hold of her wrists. "Shit. We have to stop. *You* have to stop."

Oh, *hell* no. He let her go the instant she moved her

hands, slipping loose the buckle and pulling the leather free easily. "Give me one good reason why we should," she demanded.

"Condom." He made a face. "As in, I don't have any." He sat on the mattress, tugging her between his thighs. "But trust me, I'm gonna make you feel really good before I call it a night."

"I'm sure you will." Maggie stroked his shoulders as she smiled down at him, loving the firm warmth under her fingertips. "But *you'll* feel pretty good as well—I bought a box. They're in my nightstand."

Clay pressed his forehead against her. He took a deep breath and let it out slowly, kissing her skin before looking up at her with an expression that made her knees shake. "For that you get a reward."

Moments later she was standing in front of him, dress no longer around her hips, underwear peeled away. Naked, and ready for him to be as well.

"Take off your clothes," she ordered, trying to get around him to the bed.

"No way," Clay swept her up, pausing with her breasts pressed to his heated chest. "Eventually, but this is all about you."

"About us," she insisted.

He tumbled her to the bed and crawled over her, pinning her in place with his hands beside her head, his knees on either side of her thighs. "If you don't think I'm going to enjoy this as much as you will, you have a few things to learn."

He proceeded to kiss his way down her torso, nibbling, licking and sucking as he held her hips pinned to the mattress.

Maggie leaned up on her elbows as he pushed her

thighs apart with his shoulders. He moved between them, his gaze fixed on her sex. A shiver shook her as he made contact, his fingers sliding through her folds, opening her completely.

Clay hummed in approval. "You're wet for me already. God. I can't fucking wait any longer."

Then he put his mouth on her. An electric thrill raced through her body, tingles that shot from her core outward as he licked and sucked and used his tongue in ways that made her blood rush. Heat flashed through her as he drove her toward a rapid climax.

He slipped his fingers into her. One, then another as he pumped slowly.

"More," she demanded, squirming on the spot.

He gave it to her. Easing a third finger into her core, adding pressure against her clit with his tongue. Maggie pressed her hips toward him, wanting more, needing just a little—

The fingers of his free hand ghosted over her breast, caught hold of a nipple and pinched.

Lightning struck. Her body shook, her sex squeezing tight around his fingers as he paused with them deep inside her. He slowed the motions of his tongue, moving away from the most sensitive spot, but maintaining enough pressure to drag out the rocking aftershocks until she was gasping for air.

"Stop. Stop." She laughed as she reached down to pull him over her. Clay came willingly, and he kissed her, the taste of her pleasure on his tongue as he pressed himself over her, the heavy length of his cock centered on top of her clit.

He rocked his hips slowly as he kissed her senseless.

Then he nuzzled her neck affectionately, rolling

partially off as he stroked the side of her breast as if he couldn't stop touching her. "We don't have to go any further," he murmured.

"Maybe you don't," she moaned in protest, "but I haven't had nearly enough."

Maggie rolled, and he instinctively moved with her, and they ended up with her straddling him in the middle of her king-size bed. "I have you at my mercy, exactly where I've wanted you all night."

"Exactly where I've wanted to be all night." He let out an exaggerated sigh. "Okay, fine. If you really need to ravish me, I suppose I can handle it."

She laughed before reluctantly crawling off him to grab a condom from the box. It had been years since she'd last used them, but she figured it was like riding a bicycle.

When she turned back, Clay was flat on his back, his dress pants gone. A pair of boxer briefs the only thing holding back his *enthusiasm*. "Neat magic trick."

"I thought you might want to unwrap me."

Her cheeks were beginning to hurt from her constant smile. "So nice of you to give me a present."

Maggie laid the condom on his abdomen, the flash fire in his eyes warning her she was going to get everything she needed in a very short time. Then she moved back into position over him, straddling his knees so she could lean forward and rub her cheek over his cotton-clad cock.

She got a choked gasp from him for that one.

"I think I'll take a peek." She grasped the edge of the elastic waistband with two fingers, inching back to reveal his entire length. His cock was thick and hard, rising upward as he lifted his hips so she could strip away the boxers completely.

She must've made some kind of needy noise because he

growled at her. "I'm going to explode if you keep that up," he warned.

"Hush. I'm savouring the moment."

He picked up the condom between two fingers and offered it to her. "Work while you're savouring."

Maggie opened the packet with trembling fingers and moved to place it on him, hesitating as she went to touch his cock. "I should—"

She was on her back and under him before she could finish the sentence. Clay had the condom out of her hand and rolled down, his hips pressing between hers. "You should put your legs around my hips," he ordered.

She couldn't argue with that.

Even as she caught hold, he reached down and guided his cock to her opening, slipping the head in slightly before settling back on his elbows. Straight over her, looking into her eyes.

Then without a word he pushed forward and joined them. Buried deep in one careful motion that stole her breath.

He stopped, eyes closed, sheer pleasure on his face. Maggie held on and waited, her heart pumping wildly as pleasure raced through her. Having him inside her was amazing. Having him hold her as if she was precious and beautiful—

All of it wrapped up into one incredible glow of need and desire, and she tightened around him for the joy of it.

His eyes flew open and he moaned softly. "Dammit, Maggie, I'm on the edge already here."

She pressed her lips to his skin, tugging him closer. Wanting to feel his weight over her. "Take your time. I'm in no rush."

He nuzzled her neck, hips barely moving. Just enough

to keep her anticipation high as he licked around her ear then put his teeth to the lobe and bit down softly.

A shudder shook her. "Yes."

"Hmm. Sensitive ears?"

"And my neck," she admitted readily, stroking her hands over his shoulders. Lifting her hips as much as she could as he continued to rock into her. "And my breasts—I love when you play with them."

He tilted onto one elbow, gazing down their bodies to where they joined in a lazy, controlled rhythm. "Good to know. Playing with your breasts might become my favourite thing."

Putting action to words, Clay cupped her again, pinching her nipple lightly between thumb and forefinger. Maggie pulled one leg up and tilted her hips so he would slide deeper. It had been long enough since she'd last done this that his cock stretched hard, and a little gasp escaped.

He froze. "Okay?"

She nodded vigorously, reaching for his hips and tugging them forward. "Oh, yes. Don't stop. It's good. It's *so* good."

Clay lay on his side and pulled her leg completely over his hip. The position left her wide open to his slow thrusts, and let him continue to caress her. At the same time he watched her face carefully, his breathing slowly becoming more erratic.

She curled her free hand around his back and scratched lightly. "Good?"

"Fuck, yeah," he whispered.

Maggie laughed softly. "Ready to go harder?"

Sweat beaded his forehead, but he nodded as if he weren't dying to speed up. "If you are."

She wrapped herself around him and tugged until she

ended up flat on her back, covered with a blanket of hard, sexy masculinity as he moved into her over and over. His pace increased, his thrusts going deeper, driving harder. Maggie adjusted position so she could tilt her hips and rub against his groin on every stroke, but it wasn't enough. "I need more pressure—"

Clay instantly eased to the left, licked his fingers and pressed his hand between them. Another hard thrust followed, only this time his fingers slicked over her clit and she gasped.

"Oh, yeah. Right *there*..."

As he continued to move, pleasure coiled tighter, spiraling in faster and faster. He leaned down and kissed her jaw, licking his way to where her shoulder met her neck.

He put his teeth to her skin and nipped, at the same time working her clit. Thrusting again.

She broke. "*Clay*."

An enormous pulse rocked her body, and she arched against him. He groaned, shaking as he thrust once more, then again before he too lost control and came. His hips jerked as she tightened her legs and held him inside. Heat swirled between them as pleasure flooded her veins.

Orgasms really *were* better when they were shared.

Satisfaction crept over her like the sun rising on a warm spring day as they lay tangled together, limbs askew. Clay rolled so his weight wasn't crushing her, his gaze roaming over her face.

"You look far too serious for a man who's just had an orgasm," Maggie teased, the words escaping breathlessly.

"Trust me, I'm plenty happy." He slipped away briefly and took care of the condom, pulling on his briefs before eyeing the bed. "Under the covers?"

Maggie had them pulled back in a moment, curling against his body as he resettled beside her.

She knew they had to talk. Knew there were things they had to discuss, but right then, all she wanted was to wallow in the endorphins racing through her system.

And she wanted to cuddle with the man who'd given her such pleasure. She let him get comfy before resting her head on his chest, one leg thrown over his, one arm around him in a hug.

Clay stroked his fingers through her hair, his heartbeat under her ear firm and steady.

"Just let me enjoy this for a minute, then we can talk," she murmured, soaking in his warmth and the strength of him at her side.

Their breathing synchronized, and the room faded. Only the sensation of being protected and cared for remained, and Maggie sighed with happiness.

And fell sleep.

CHAPTER 10

C lay stroked her softly, stared at the ceiling and wondered what the hell he was going to do.

He couldn't stay. Not without a shit-ton of consequences he didn't think Maggie was ready for. But he couldn't leave—didn't *want* to leave.

But then it didn't matter what he wanted, not really. No way on earth would he be selfish enough to let her get any backlash after what had been amazing sex, *fucking* amazing sex, at least in his opinion.

He waited until she was sound asleep before carefully untangling himself and stealing from the bed. Maggie rolled after him, her fingers spread over the warm spot where his body had been, and he stared at her for a moment.

Her eyes remained closed, the faintest hint of a smile on her lips. He pulled up the blankets and leaned in to kiss her cheek before grabbing his clothes from the floor. One soft *click* later and the bedside light extinguished, then he silently snuck out of the room.

Clay dressed in the hallway—the only place he knew for certain there were no windows and that his shadow wouldn't be seen. Then he went through the rest of the house and turned off most of the lights before pulling on his outer layers and heading out, locking the door behind him.

It was just after midnight when he got in his truck, the outdoor light on Maggie's house shining faintly on the trail of his footprints left in the new snow that had started when they'd left the party.

As he drove off he noticed a curtain fall into place on one of the homes across the street, and sighed. Bloody busybodies. Hopefully they'd chalk it up to another night where he'd stayed to watch a movie.

He certainly wasn't ashamed to be involved with Maggie, but until they had hammered out the details he'd do anything to keep her safe.

Only when he got home and walked into his cold, lonely bedroom a whole lot of *who gives a fuck* began rolling through his brain. Shit, he was smarter than this. Hell if he couldn't have his cake and eat it too.

Clay tossed clean clothes into a small bag and trotted back to his truck, taking the long way around to Janey and Len's house which was a heck of a lot closer to Maggie's.

He parked in the back, turning off the motor as quickly as he could before climbing from behind the wheel and pacing silently up the walkway.

A light was on in the kitchen. His brother Len stared out the window, and while Clay didn't want to get into a lengthy discussion, he also didn't want this to go any further. If he had to beg for help, he would.

Yet without a word spoken, Len offered him a grin. He pressed a finger over his lips and like a kid, mimed throwing away a key.

Len was no dummy, and he was observant. He'd obviously put two and two together without any help on Clay's part, which was a good thing *and* a warning. If Len had figured it out so quickly, others would as well, and while his brother would remain silent, Clay doubted they'd get the same consideration from others in the community.

But that wasn't what he wanted to dwell on tonight. He gave his brother a brisk salute then jogged past his truck. He slipped down alleyways for the couple of blocks it took to reach Maggie's back door, pulling out the hidden key he'd been shown him so long ago, and let himself in.

The house was quiet, and Clay moved quickly in the darkness, stripping down to his briefs in the guest room. He rubbed his hands together to warm them up then returned to the master bedroom.

Maggie had changed position and was curled around a pillow, her face relaxed as she slept. The signs of her loss were there in the small lines that had formed at the edges of her eyes, but Clay thought she was the most beautiful woman he'd ever seen.

He crawled back into bed and pulled her against him. Spooning her hips to his groin, wrapping an arm around her body. She tilted her head toward him, and he didn't resist. He pressed a kiss to her cheek, to her jaw, and a happy sigh escaped her.

Touching her turned him on, but getting to simply hold her was the whole reason he'd gone through the elaborate ruse tonight. Clay closed his eyes and ignored the world of problems about to rain down on their heads and simply savoured where he was.

It was the warmth that woke her.

Maggie's head rested on a firm set of biceps, her fingers

linked with Clay's where their hands lay against her naked stomach.

In some other world, or at some other time, she might've worried about not having the flattest tummy, or about morning breath, or any of those things that made waking up naked with someone new embarrassing.

Or maybe she should have been thinking about Cameron, the only other man she'd ever had in her bed. Should she feel guilt? Sadness?

No matter how much she tried, though, the only emotion bubbling through her veins was happiness. Right now? Felt amazing, and she wasn't going to waste a single second of it worrying.

Cameron would have wanted her to enjoy life, and she was pretty sure he would have approved of Clay, all things considered.

She was wide-awake, completely rested for the first time in what felt like forever. Behind her, Clay's even breathing told her he was still snoozing, and she resisted the urge to wiggle against him.

He'd wake up soon enough, because while *he* might not be awake, other parts of his anatomy were already prepping for the morning.

Maggie stifled a giggle. God, morning wood was one of those things she and Cameron had joked about so often over the years. It might be perfectly natural, but as far as she was concerned it was also *perfect*.

That whole bit about her enjoying sex—morning sex was her favourite.

She lasted another ten whole minutes, watching the sun inch its way across the snow-covered branches outside the bedroom window. The clock wasn't visible from this angle, but she guessed it had to be at least six a.m.

Early birds really did get to enjoy the best part of the day.

Unable to resist temptation any longer, Maggie adjusted her hips, settling a little tighter to his hard-on.

And...his breathing changed. Between one second and the next Clay woke up. He seemed to pause, as if wondering if she was okay with their intimate positioning.

Okay? She wanted to get a whole lot more intimate.

She twisted her head as she leaned against his chest, and he lifted slightly until he could look down at her. "Hey."

"Hey, yourself." Maggie waggled her brows. "You're so kind. You brought me a present."

Confusion drifted over his gaze.

She bit her lower lip to hold back her laughter. Okay, so he wasn't the type who woke up firing on all cylinders. She tugged her fingers free from his then reached over her hip, adjusting position enough to reach between them and run her fingers over his solid length.

Clay sucked for air. "Oh."

"Oh, *yes*?"

He grinned and shifted his hands lower as well, moving until his palm rested possessively over her mound. "I think we can work something out."

She found herself being rolled backward, the thick ridge of his cock pressing against her butt cheek as he draped her over him. The hand between her legs moved carefully, one thick finger stroking her clit in small circles.

With his other hand he made it clear he'd been listening last night as he played with her breasts. His caresses were brief and gentle, more teasing at first than anything else, but combined with what else he was doing, pleasure languidly built in her core.

"Hmm, this is a nice way to start the day." Her words were all but a purr. She liked being petted and cared for. Had missed it, desperately. Only she felt a little selfish. "I can't touch you in this position," she complained.

Clay's nose bumped her ear, his deep voice a rumble against her throat. "You don't need to touch me. Trust me, I'm having a great time. Just relax."

She hummed happily. "Next time, I get to pick the position."

She couldn't see his face but by the skip in his breathing and the increase in tempo of his fingers, Clay had no objection to her suggestion. She rocked her hips against him, getting a little action in against his cock. He growled and caught hold of her earlobe, sucking it into his mouth and tormenting her with tiny nips and brief sucks along her neck.

A flutter of need, aching desire—it built slowly this time, and as a pulse of pleasure rocked through her, Maggie arched against his hand and let him drag out the sensation for as long as possible.

Her breathing was uneven and her limbs loose as he placed her on her stomach. She watched through a haze of satisfaction as he took a condom from the box and rolled it on, his brown eyes focused on her.

Then he crawled over her and pinned her down, pressing his lips to the back of her neck. "I take it that means I get to pick our position?"

"Gee, I wonder what you've decided?" Maggie teased.

His cock was a heavy weight resting between her legs, and he lifted her hips higher, thrusting forward and rubbing the hot length over her sensitive clit. It felt wonderful. It felt amazing, but it wasn't enough.

She tilted her hips the next time he moved, and the head of his cock breached her folds.

He sucked for air, his voice trembling as he spoke. "You're fucking killing me. Was that your plan?"

"I hoped *your* plan was to fuck me," she said around the smile that could not be repressed. Another wiggle of her hips inched him farther inside her, and his expression tightened.

A man fighting for control—way to stroke a woman's ego. Maggie arched back harder and pushed her hips toward him, burying his length in her in one firm motion.

This time she was the one who gasped with pleasure.

A slow stream of soft curses escaped his lips as Clay held on tightly to her hips and withdrew. She closed her eyes and soaked in the sensation of being filled completely as he moved forward. Rocking into her with deliberate, careful motions.

Her entire body tingled, and she snuck her hand under her belly and between her legs, touching where he entered her. Wetting her fingers in the moisture between them. Touching his cock as he pulled back because she could, the intimacy jolting her heart with an extra pulse.

"I'm ready for more," she said as she brought her fingers to her clit and rubbed.

Clay moved again, but careful and controlled. "So fucking beautiful. God, you feel so good around me. You touching yourself?"

She nodded. "Uh-huh. And it feels great, but I want more. Take me harder," she demanded.

He faltered for a second, gripping her hips tightly before he relaxed his hands and smoothed his palms over her ass cheeks. "Nope," he refused. "Come on my cock," he ordered instead. "You come, and then I'll fuck you harder."

She wasn't sure if she should be pissed off or frustrated, but she was having such a good time, there wasn't really anything to complain about. Instead she increased the tempo over her clit, pushing back against him so that every time he thrust, her butt hit his groin.

A half dozen times later and she trembled on the verge of climax, fingers clenching the bed sheet as she squeezed around him.

His fingers tightened as he sped up just that bit she needed. "Clay. Oh, *yes...*"

Everything tightened. Heck, the sheets protested under her fingers, the wicked and wonderful sensation of being completely filled as her body clenched around his hard shaft rocking her. That was what was wonderful. That was what made her shudder in pleasure.

And so much for Clay doing anything more—he came on the heels of her orgasm, a cry of pleasure escaping his lips as he pressed her to the mattress and buried himself as deep as possible.

Her sex pulsed around him as his cock jerked inside her. His chest rubbed against her back as he breathed rapidly, his arms on either side of her trembling.

"God, I love this morning," she sighed with satisfaction.

Clay chuckled, pressing a kiss under her ear. "Don't go anywhere," he ordered before dealing with the condom, returning to her side and wrapping himself around her.

Sunshine poured in the bedroom window, falling across them on the messed-up sheets. Maggie twisted to face him, trailing her fingers through his messy hair and pushing it off his forehead.

"I keep expecting to wake up and find out this is all a dream."

He grinned. "Want me to pinch you?"

His fingers drifted over her ass, and she squirmed away. "No, don't."

More laughter ensued as he captured her and dragged her back and started over, kissing and nuzzling at her neck until her entire body quivered.

"We're not going to get out of bed all day if you keep that up," she told him happily.

His answering sigh was unexpected.

She caught his face in her hands and turned him toward her. All the amusement and passion from only moments earlier had faded.

Drat. The one thing she didn't want to happen. "You've got that look in your eyes. The one that says we shouldn't have done this."

"Hell, no." He shook his head. "Don't think for a second I regret last night, or this morning, but..."

"...but you think we shouldn't have done this," she finished for him, rolling away to a sitting position. She grabbed her sleep shirt from under the pillow and pulled it over her head, the oversized Calgary Stampeders jersey a more than adequate barrier between them.

She wasn't running away, but she wasn't about to have a serious discussion with her naked boobs involved in the conversation.

Clay sighed, capturing her hands in his to keep her at his side. "No. I don't regret any of it, and I hope you want more. And I'm not just talking about sex, although, yes I want that too."

It was Maggie's turn to pause. She'd given this a lot of thought before making a move on him, but she'd deliberately avoided dwelling on some parts of the problem. Like what would come next.

It hadn't been worth borrowing trouble before she even knew if he was interested. But now...

Where did they go with this?

"What you mean, you want more?" she asked cautiously.

Clay trailed his fingers up her arm, watching as they moved. "This wasn't just sex, Mags. I care about you, and I like you."

She snorted. Very elegant, but impossible to stop. "I hope you like me, dumbass."

His smile flashed, and he threaded his fingers into the hair at the back of her head. "It does sound funny, doesn't it? But I mean it. I think we're friends."

They weren't the words she wanted to say but they snuck out anyway. "Friends with benefits?"

An expression of complete horror rolled over him. "No. *Never* that."

Good. "I hate that phrase."

He nodded. "Me too. Friends, definitely. Sex, well—"

He waggled his brows, and she giggled like a teenager before answering, "Sex, *definitely*." And now the concern was back on his face, so Maggie straight-out asked him. "Why are you so worried?"

He paused. "I have no problem with us just being us, but that's not going to be enough. Not for this community. Not for the other people out there."

She wasn't stupid, but it seemed as if he was making it a bigger problem than it would be. "It's not really anybody else's business."

"I agree," he said with a sharp nod. "Only what do we tell them? Are we dating?"

"You want to?" she asked in return.

"Hell, yeah," Clay responded instantly. "Only..."

His phone rang. The same dirty sexually provocative ringtone as before, and they paused for a split second before breaking out laughing, both from the tension of the moment and from shared memories.

"Hold that thought," Clay ordered as he scrambled off the bed and into the next room, returning to the master bedroom as he answered the call. "Clay Thompson."

His eyes widened briefly before he rolled them, placing a finger to his lips. They weren't done talking, so Maggie leaned against the headboard and waited.

"Yes, Mrs. Pfeiffer. The shop will be open on Monday at eight a.m. like usual. Unless this is an emergency..."

Clay settled on the bed by her feet, holding the phone against his ear with his shoulder and picking up her feet so he could rub them.

Man, oh, man. Whatever "this" was they were doing, Maggie suddenly wanted a heck of a lot more of it.

"No, Mrs. Pfeiffer. You're not interrupting anything. But it's Sunday, and unless you want to pay extra for emergency services, you should contact the shop during normal working hours." He listened for a little longer, his frustration growing, but none of it bleeding into his voice as he spoke. "You phoned my private line."

The thin sound of an older woman's voice escaped his phone, and Maggie already guessed what Clay would tell her once he got off the line.

So she needed to know what she was going to say. What *did* she want?

The closet in the corner of the room was partially opened, Cameron's clothes hanging neatly on one side. There were more of his things around the house because she hadn't been ready to get rid of them yet.

But she was getting *closer* to being ready.

Was it too soon to be officially involved with another man? Maybe, but a very smart part inside of her said she *wasn't* getting involved with a stranger. This was *Clay*. This was her friend, and he'd already owned a piece of her heart.

It didn't mean she knew exactly what she wanted in the future, but she knew what she wanted right now.

Clay hung up the phone and went back to massaging her feet.

"Gossip-mongers?" Maggie asked innocently.

"I bet after last night someone wondered if there was hanky-panky going on between us." He wiggled the phone in the air. "...and that's why I'm worried."

She snuck her feet out of his hands and slid forward, straddling his thighs. "You know what? We don't need a name for this. We don't need a name for *us*. We're friends, first and foremost, and whatever else is happening between us is our business. Let people talk if they want to—there's nothing we can do to stop that, anyway."

"I don't want anyone to hurt you," Clay said softly.

His concern was understandable and yet so out of place in her reality. She'd lost her husband and her best friend. *That* was pain. *That* was hurting so hard she'd barely been able to breathe.

Clay? Made her breathe again. Anyone who wanted to judge her for that could take a flying leap off a tall building.

"Nobody can hurt me with their silly words or judgments," Maggie insisted. "I'll be honest with you. I might not know exactly what we're doing, but what we're doing isn't wrong. Deep down inside me I know that, and I'm good with us. With whatever 'us' is."

He nodded, his sexy grin curling back into place even though a touch of doubt lingered in his eyes. "Then I'm good with it too."

She bounced out of his lap before he could reach for her. Morning sex? No problem. Morning kisses? "Not before I brush my teeth," she insisted.

"Uh-oh, here come the rules." Clay followed, swatting her on the butt as he passed by on the way to the bag he'd left by the door. "Sounds like we're dating to me."

She didn't need a label for it. She really didn't. "Plans for the day?" she asked.

"You okay going over to Len and Janey's for lunch?"

"I had nothing scheduled. Sure."

Clay cleared his throat. "Good, then lets wing it for the morning. See what *comes up...*"

His cheesy smile made it impossible to not offer him one in return before he headed to the guest bathroom. Happiness swirled around her.

And after they'd both gotten minty fresh her second present of the day arrived. Kisses that made her head spin and her body heat until she was breathless and giddy and ready to be tumbled back into bed all over.

Luckily, Clay had the same agenda.

CHAPTER 11

Clay bet anything he was wearing the stupidest smirk ever, but damn if he could stop himself. He paced down the back alley, Maggie at his side. She was telling him about the plants she'd ordered for the Habitat project, and he was listening, really he was.

But mostly what he was doing was buzzing with satisfaction. It had been a hell of a great morning, in every way possible.

And when she stepped closer and slipped her fingers into his, something rolled in his gut, and the beautiful April day turned even brighter.

He knocked once on the door at his brother's before opening it and shouting a greeting. The smell of coffee and bacon wafted toward them, and his stomach grumbled. They hadn't made it to the eating portion of the day yet, too distracted with other things.

Clay grinned harder.

Janey stuck her head around the corner. "Hey, guys. Come in and make yourself at home. Len's burning the bacon, and I need to supervise."

"I'm not burning anything," Len muttered in the background. "Get your ass back here before the eggs turn to rubber."

Clay took Maggie's coat and hung it on one of the half-dozen hooks lining the wall in the mudroom. Stupid how much satisfaction he got out of draping his coat over hers.

"Did they know we were coming?" Maggie whispered, leaning her shoulder against him as she spoke.

It was one of those opportunities he wasn't going to miss. He slipped his arms around her waist and pulled her closer. She settled in tight, hands resting lightly on his chest as she looked up expectantly. "I texted him," Clay admitted.

A brief cough interrupted them. Janey stood in the doorway. "What do you guys want to drink?"

Clay braced himself for Maggie to pull away, or jerk back in surprise at being caught cuddled up intimately, but she didn't budge. Just swung her head toward Janey and answered. "Coffee is good."

"Me too."

Then the fire alarm went off and Janey's eyes widened. She whirled out of sight as the aroma of bacon took on a decidedly charcoaly tinge. Laughter and smoke poured from the kitchen along with the sound of windows being opened and what maybe was chairs being dragged over the floor.

Maggie's nose wrinkled as she smiled at him. "Good thing we don't work as undercover agents. We suck at keeping secrets."

"We don't need to hide anything around these two. I'd already thought about that," Clay admitted.

"Of course you had." She tapped him on the chest then moved toward the stairway and up the couple risers into the kitchen. The shrieking siren cut off as Clay followed hard on her heels.

Len stood on a kitchen chair, the fire alarm open above his head and the disconnected battery in his hand. Janey cautiously carried a cookie sheet in her oven-mitted hands. "Coming through," she shouted, aiming for the back door.

Clay went ahead of her and pushed aside the screen door so she could go outside to drop the still-smoking pan on the picnic table on the back deck.

Still, she was chuckling when they returned to the kitchen, Len sheepishly replacing the chair at the table.

It took a little juggling but they ended up with a decent brunch, no bacon, the four of them gathered around the table sharing comfortable conversation.

He watched for any signs that Maggie was feeling uncomfortable, but she and Janey seemed to have a lot to discuss, so he poured himself another cup of coffee and sat back to enjoy the meal.

Len knocked his elbow lightly to get his attention. "Not that you have to tell me anything, but..."

He tilted his head toward the girls. They were looking over a photo album Janey had brought to the table full of highlights from housing projects she'd completed. Maggie was smiling with enthusiasm as she asked questions.

Clay spoke softly, not disturbing their animated discussion. "Not much to tell yet."

His brother stirred his coffee slowly. "No problem. Let me know if there's anything you need."

It was a strange offer in many ways. Clay was used to being the one who took care of his family, not the one who leaned on them for help. And yet he was so close to the situation, it would be good to get an outside opinion.

"You're okay with it?"

Len glanced at him, his expression unreadable. "Doesn't bug me. Just don't know how it's gonna go over around town."

Which echoed exactly what Clay was worried about. "Yeah."

And he was back to being stuck in that position between personally not giving a damn what the collective busybodies thought, and wanting to protect Maggie from more pain. Yet...she'd said she was fine with it. He had to respect that, as hard as it was.

"As long as you guys are there for us, that's all we need," Clay admitted.

Len bumped his fist into Clay's shoulder, and it was the only answer he got. But from his brother, that was more than enough assurance.

"What are you guys up to for the rest of the day?" Janey asked.

Maggie glanced at him. "We didn't talk about it yet."

A repeat of their morning sounded good to Clay, but he could control himself for a few hours. Spend some time in the fresh air before he took her back to bed. "How about a tour at the project site? Want to see how it's coming along?"

"Hey, that's a great idea." Janey pushed back from the table and grabbed the rest of the dirty dishes to pile them in the sink. "I haven't seen it since you guys took down the old buildings."

"I need to get changed and put on my boots," Maggie said. "I can meet you there."

He wasn't letting her get away that easily. "*We'll* meet you there," Clay told Len.

He helped her into his truck, once again guiding her through the driver side. Maggie settled in the middle, laughing softly as she waved goodbye to Janey.

"What?" Clay asked. "What's so funny?"

"You. Did you really hide your truck here last night?"

"Hey, it seemed like a brilliant idea at one in the morning."

She laughed again. "I'm sure it did. It was more than I could think up at that time, but really, it's not necessary. We're grownups, and if we're going to do this, I'm not ducking around corners like I'm ashamed to be seen with you."

He didn't answer until he pulled into her driveway and put the truck in park. Then before she could escape out the passenger door he caught her chin in his fingers, staring into her unwavering gaze. Such a beautiful, strong woman. "Ashamed is the *last* thing I am. I'm so fucking amazed you want to have anything to do with me. I mean that."

The edges of her lips curled into a smile. "Are you coming in while I get changed?"

"Tempting, but we promised we'd meet Len and Janey soon." He pushed open the door and helped her down, keeping her fingers linked in his as he walked her to the door. "Get changed—I'll wait here."

CLAY DROVE SLOWLY past the building site. "When was the last time you were here?" he asked, his fingers warm where he'd refused to let go of hers.

"A couple of weeks ago. Before you guys took down the hall." Maggie leaned forward to peer out the window, eager to check out the changes. "At this stage of the game there's not a lot for me to do, so I'm making sure I don't get in anybody's way."

"It's neat to see the progress." He pointed to the small

shed that had been constructed at the edge of the rectangular lot. "Like that. They built it yesterday. It's full of construction equipment, but you'll be able to take it over after they're done. It will be a good place to store gardening tools."

She nodded eagerly, slipping out of her seatbelt the instant he stopped. There was a skiff of snow on the ground and the air felt more like winter than spring, but seeing the lot without the old ramshackle hall made it seem a lot more real.

"I can hardly wait until the buildings start to go up."

Clay didn't answer. He was moving toward where Len and Janey stood near the corner fence. Maggie followed, wondering why they were stomping in circles.

She got close enough for the reason to become clear and jerked to a stop. "Oh, no."

Janey pulled a face, rubbing her heel harder over a small fire, leaving a black streak behind. "Some bored kids, I guess. Lighting grass fires."

"And doing some decorating." Len shook his head. "So damn stupid. They've got the youth center just around the corner. Why the heck were they hanging out here?"

Maggie moved toward the fence where someone had taken a couple of cans of spray paint and written obscenities. It wasn't artistic graffiti; it was straight-out ugly. "Daniel said some of the older kids were using the hall as a hangout. I guess they're not happy about losing the space."

"Doesn't excuse them acting like idiots," Clay turned on the spot and swore. "Or breaking into things they shouldn't."

Maggie followed his gaze to the new shed. From this angle it was clear that the neat miniature barn-shaped building had also suffered unwanted attention. On the backside, the pristine red wood with its neat white trim was covered with more spray paint, a violent scar against the pretty freshness.

While Clay and Len dealt with the broken window, Janey linked her arm through Maggie's and pulled her in another direction. "Come on, there's nothing we can do, and if I know the guys, they're just holding back out of consideration for our delicate ears."

"So we should walk away and let them cuss a bit?" Maggie asked.

Janey shrugged. "We have different ways of coping. Our guys have a few rough edges. At times it seems Len likes to think he's guarding some princess in a castle, but it doesn't hurt anything for me to let him."

Maggie walked silently for a moment. Her brain had stuttered to a stop at *our guys*. She cleared her throat. "We kind of threw this at you this morning. Me and Clay, I mean. But you didn't seem upset."

"Are you kidding me? Len warned me not to overwhelm you with gushing enthusiasm. I think you and Clay getting together is awesome."

It was good to have another supporter. "Good."

"Right. But if he does anything to hurt you? I will nail his balls to the floor."

Janey's obviously well-intended yet bloodthirsty comment made Maggie laugh. "Remind me not to get on your bad side."

"Hey, there are more of them in this family than us. Guys, I mean, so we need to stick together." Janey squeezed her arm, pulling them to a stop at the end of the lot where they could look back over the entire section. "Really. I like you because you're an amazing woman, and that's not gonna change."

A warm glow rose fast. "Thank you."

She wasn't sure what else to say. And then she realized, at this point she didn't have to. She was finding new friends, and new activities to fill the void left behind by Cameron's passing.

She was living again. One day at a time.

CHAPTER 12

Maggie grumbled as she stared at the closet where neat stacks of clothing thumbed their nose at her. That whole complaining about having nothing to wear—that woman had never been her, but suddenly it *was* her.

Clay had suggested they go out for dinner then hit Traders for some dancing, and here it was barely two in the afternoon, and she was already fussing about her clothes.

She was torn. Should she dress casual as if this were just another outing between two good friends, or put on something a little special? She was leaning toward something that would make that sexy look of appreciation light up his eyes.

Only her wardrobe was sadly lacking. A lot of things didn't fit anymore since she'd lost weight. Some things she didn't want to wear because they'd been Cameron's favourites, and while it shouldn't matter, it did.

Her gaze drifted to the other side of the closet where most of his things still hung. It made no sense to keep them, not when other people could use them.

Maggie deliberately went to the kitchen and grabbed a bunch of plastic bags along with a sharpie. She split his work clothes and a couple of dressier outfits into bags for some of the older boys at school who she knew could use them, hoping she could find a way to pass on the items without hurting their masculine pride.

Then she went through *her* things ruthlessly, chucking the more sentimental ones into a bag for charity outside Rocky Mountain House area. She didn't want to turn the corner at the grocery store and spot someone wearing a familiar outfit. It wasn't that big of a deal, but there was no reason why she had to set herself up for pain.

By the time she'd gone through the entire collection, her bed was covered and most of her closet was empty, and she was debating having a good old-fashioned pity-party for an hour or so.

Of course, that's when Clay walked in.

He took one look at the stacks and another at her face then damn if he didn't just swoop in and gather her up. Holding her tight and offering comfort.

If she hadn't wanted to cry before, his tender touch would've been enough to set her off. This time it wasn't heart-wrenching body-shaking sobs, which she was thankful for. She had done enough of that in the early days to never want to get that upset again. But it was impossible to stop the tears washing down her cheeks as she clutched the front of his shirt and hid in the circle of his arms.

It took a little while before she could steady her breathing enough to speak without sounding like a fool. "I didn't hear you come in. I'm so sorry."

He didn't move, just kept stroking her back. "I knocked, but when you didn't come to the door I let myself in. What on earth are you apologizing for?"

She rested her forehead against his chest, fingertips moving slowly over the fabric of his T-shirt. "I feel horrid. So often when you come over, you have to mop me up."

Clay caught her chin in his fingers and tilted her head back until there was nowhere for her to look except straight into his eyes. His gaze trapped her and held her captive. "Don't you *ever* regret letting me see what you're feeling. You don't need to hide your emotions from me."

"Missing him hits out of nowhere at times, and suddenly I'm a mess. It's got to be a tough reminder for you as well."

He made a noise somewhere between a growl of frustration and a rumble of pain. "Cam was a good friend, and I miss him like hell, but that doesn't mean I know what you're going through, so don't you ever apologize for that again."

Maggie swallowed around the lump in her throat and forced a nod. "Why did I guess you'd say that?"

Clay smoothed his fingers through her hair, a soft smile returning to his lips. "Because you know I'm a fabulous guy, and that's what us fabulous guys do. I have a question for you—a serious one."

Maggie stepped out of his embrace and took a deep breath, wiping the tears from her cheeks as she pulled herself together. "Shoot."

He tilted his head toward the kitchen. "What say we order ourselves a pizza tonight? We can check what's on Netflix and have a quiet evening, just the two of us."

Sudden relief rolled through her. The last thing she wanted tonight was to put on a happy face and head out on the town. "I should've figured you'd say that, too," Maggie admitted. "It sounds wonderful, if you really don't mind."

"Nope, not one bit. Although, at some point I do want to take you dancing."

She accepted the hand he held toward her. "You just want another chance to grope me in public," she teased.

"Maybe," he confessed. "Although groping you in private is a lot more interesting."

Before they left the room, she glanced back at the bed. She'd come so far; she hated to give up on her task. "Once we order the pizza, can you can help me finish this?"

Clay nodded, his expression serious as his strong fingers wrapped around hers. It was another task to get through and to get beyond.

It was a whole lot easier because he was there.

By the time pizza arrived, all the bags had been carried outside and placed in Clay's truck. He promised to drop them off at the appropriate charity boxes. With two large pizzas on the table and a movie on the TV, Maggie settled in next to him. He ate one-handed, his other arm draped around her shoulders as if he wanted to keep her close. She finished a couple slices and then curled in tighter, resting her head against his chest.

She wasn't even sure what they were watching because it was more about being there with a warm body at her side. Someone who was so much more than just a friend, and impulsively she tilted her head back and pressed her lips against his cheek.

Clay glanced at her and offered a smile. "What was that for?"

Maggie shrugged, laying her hand on top of his arm. "Thank you for being you. I don't know how I would've made it through without your help."

He leaned closer and pressed his lips to hers for a brief second. A kiss of tenderness and compassion and friendship all wrapped up in one. When he pulled back, his eyes shone with happiness. "No problem, Mags. I like being there for you."

CHAPTER 13

Before he could get out of the truck, Maggie was already darting down the front steps and jerking open the passenger door.

She climbed in and offered him a kiss.

"You're ready bright and early," he said with a chuckle.

Maggie sat back to do up her seatbelt. "Hey, it's been a long time since I've been shopping in Red Deer. I'm a little giddy."

Clay shook his head in amusement. "If this trip makes you giddy, just wait till we do the drive to Calgary." He eyed the space between them. "You really going to sit all the way over there?"

Maggie laughed as she undid her seatbelt and moved into the center of the bench seat. "Bossy."

She had no idea how much he was holding back. Clay laid a hand on her thigh and drove with the other, heading them out of town. "I promised you shopping and lunch. You okay with us being back in time for dinner? Katy wants everyone to come on over for my dad's birthday tonight instead of tomorrow."

She nodded. "Not a problem at all, in fact we don't even have to go today—"

"Enough," he interrupted. "We've tried to get away two weekends in a row. This time we're going."

She settled in beside him, her complaining done, and Clay relaxed and enjoyed having her tucked up against him.

They'd been together officially for nearly four weeks, although it had to be one of the slowest-boil relationships he'd ever seen. They were used to spending time with each other, and in some ways that familiarity was setting the pace. He went over to her place, or she came over to his, and suddenly it seemed as if there were always at least a couple of his family around.

It had never really registered how much he saw of the lot of them outside of work hours. The closeness wasn't something he wanted to change, but it did make finding alone time more challenging.

He also didn't want Maggie to think the only reason he was with her was for sex. Although, holy *hell*, the times they'd found themselves alone, they'd both been more than eager to let loose.

"I made a list of the shops I want to check, and most of them are at the mall. You drop me off, and we'll arrange a place to meet in a few hours."

Clay glanced at her in confusion. "Why would I do that? I'm going to be with you."

"Right." She stared out the window at the passing fields, amusement in her voice.

"I'm serious. I said I was taking you shopping—of course I'm staying with you."

It was her turn to look confused as she lifted big green eyes to meet his, a shadow of sorrow slipping in like it always did when she mentioned her husband. "Cameron

135

hated shopping with a passion. He always had his own list of things to do."

Clay shrugged, gently turning the conversation to another good memory best he could. "I know. He used to complain about it sometimes, but in a nice way. About how *his girl needed her frills and things*."

Her laugh was shaky, but she was smiling again. "Yeah, he did get a kick out of some of the stuff I spent time on, so seriously, I don't expect you to waste your morning babysitting me."

For once *she* wasn't listening. "Maggie. Unless you don't want me along for some reason, my morning's entertainment *is* shopping with you."

"Seriously?"

"Yup."

She leaned against the seat looking at him as if he'd sprouted green fur. "That's not very guy-like."

Clay hit the turn indicator to change lanes then set the cruise control for the rest of their travel time on the highway. "After Mom died, I was in charge of a lot of things, including making sure everybody had decent clothes to wear. The guys were easy, although Troy bitched a lot about getting hand-me-downs, but Katy?" He shook his head at the memory. "It's as if she knew I couldn't say no to her, not with her being the only girl after four boys. She was the one who got new-to-us stuff, although a lot of it came from the thrift shop. But even then she would make it into an event, and I'd end up hauling her and Janey out shopping on a Saturday for a couple of hours."

"Oh lord, really?" She squeezed his fingers where they were linked with hers. "I was around for a year after you lost your mom. You guys seemed to take things in stride for the most part. I mean, I knew you were sad, but you were always at school, and Katy especially seemed okay."

"We all watched out for her. And my brothers stepped up, for the most part. He won't admit it, but Len did all the laundry for years, and Mitch more than pulled his weight in the shop. Troy—well, Troy was Troy."

"And you went shopping with the girls."

He nodded. "I couldn't drop them off because they were just kids, but also because Katy demanded she show me everything she tried on so I could pronounce it 'princess worthy' or not."

Maggie relaxed against him, a true smile flitting across her lips. "Fine. Since you've been well trained, I have no objections to you joining me. My list is short and simple, so if you need to pick anything up, we'll have time for you as well."

As they wandered through the mall together, Clay wondered at her definition of *short and simple*. They walked in and out of every store in the mall, and the collection of bags he carried grew steadily.

Only she was having so much fun he didn't have the heart to tease. Instead he smiled and nodded as she grabbed things off the rack and disappeared to try them on.

The first time she stepped out of the change room and waved at him he'd hurried across the store to fix what was wrong.

She'd pulled on a flirty sundress with butterflies flitting across the hemline.

Clay dragged his gaze off her legs and forced himself to focus on her face. "What's up?"

Maggie twirled, that damn skirt rising even higher to taunt him. When they both landed back in place, she was smiling hard. "Is it princess worthy?"

A laugh escaped as he pulled her against his body and dropped a kiss on her lips. "Nope. There's nothing little girl about you, and I like that just fine."

They tucked the bags in the truck before enjoying a late lunch then hitting the highway home. By the time they reached the outskirts of Rocky Mountain House, dinner hour was close.

"Is there time to change?" Maggie asked.

Clay glanced at his watch. "Barely. I'll drop you off, run home, and come back to get you."

She made a rude noise. "Why don't you wear the new things you bought? You can change at my place."

Tempting, but...

"That would only make us later," he admitted.

Fire flashed in her eyes, and the responding ache in his body made it even more difficult to stick to his plans. And when he picked her up and she was wearing that damn sundress, the only thing that kept him heading the right direction was the fact his family knew how to find him.

Not showing up for his dad's birthday party? They'd never live it down.

The instant they stopped in front of the house, Katy peeked her head out the front door and shouted at them. "Anna goes on shift in half an hour, so we're doing the cake and presents first. Get your butts in here."

They walked into a room full of pent-up energy. The girls had hung streamers from the ceiling to the lights, and he supposed it was supposed to look festive. It looked more like a spider web, but Clay held his tongue and headed to where his dad sat in the seat of honour, his grandson on his lap. "What's this nonsense about you getting older?"

"Older, but not wiser," Keith teased back, his smile falling on Maggie. "Hello, Margaret. Good to see you."

"You too, Mr. Thompson. Happy birthday." She stepped forward to offer him the card and cookies she'd bought that afternoon. "I hope there's a wonderful year ahead for you."

Keith stood and gave her a hug, then pointed at the chair next to him. "Sit down and you can take over this young man for me."

Maggie accepted Tanner and sat on the edge of the loveseat, smiling at Katy as she brought in plates and forks, dodging around her brothers. "If he fusses, don't take it personally," Katy warned, "He's teething and a grumpy butt because of it."

Clay let the sounds of his family drift past as he held out his present to his father. "You're so damn hard to buy for."

"Ha. You got me the same thing as last year, didn't you?" Keith tugged the bag from his fingers and peeked inside. "Good to know some things never change."

"Dad," Katy scolded. "Wait for everyone to get here before you start opening stuff."

"It's a subscription to a car magazine, Katy. Your brother's bought me one since he was ten years old."

Still, he put aside the bag obediently and waited for the big moment. Clay made his way across to sit next to Maggie, giving Tanner a poke in the tummy and making faces at him until his nephew offered a gap-toothed grin.

"Happy birthday to you..."

Everyone in the room picked up the refrain as Janey carried in an oversized birthday cake and settled it in front of Keith. The singing was out of tune, but enthusiastic, and the cheering when Keith blew out the candles echoed off the walls of the small house.

Presents and cake and the babble from the gathering

wrapped around Clay like a familiar blanket. He leaned back and eased his arm around Maggie as he watched his family. Troy and Mitch pretended to wrestle for the last of the icing roses on the top of the cake, and Maggie whispered in his ear, "Isn't Troy seeing someone? I thought she might be here today."

Clay pulled back in surprise. He answered softly as well, his lips brushing a lock of hair that had escaped her ponytail. "As far as I know Troy's fancy-free and happily playing the field."

She looked so confused for a moment it was utterly adorable, and he couldn't resist kissing her briefly.

Her cheeks flushed but she smiled then leaned around him to answer the shouted query to her name from across the room. Clay watched her join in the conversation, her body warm against his, and let his gaze drift over the room.

It stuttered to a stop on his father who was no longer smiling or teasing anyone. His face had gone completely white, and he was staring at the wall as if he'd seen a ghost.

God, was he having a heart attack?

Before Clay could check to be sure he was okay, Keith stood and marched across the room, offering a farewell hug to Anna before she pulled on her RCMP coat over her uniform. Then he vanished into the bathroom.

Clay was ready to pound down the door and ask some awkward questions, only dinner was announced and his dad reappeared in time to gather at the table.

Conversation was quick and steady as usual, except for Keith being more reserved.

Katy noticed it too. "You okay, Dad?"

He nodded. "Just tired.

"That's what happens when you get old," Troy said around a mouthful of pie. "—hey, watch it."

Mitch had smacked him across the back of the head. "Oops, I meant 'pass the whipped cream'."

"You know what? I'm going to go home early and get some rest. You kids carry-on without me." Keith tilted his head toward the apartment he lived in over the shop. "Help me take my presents back to my place," he snapped at Clay.

Clay wasn't sure why he was being ordered around in that tone, or why his dad needed help with a handful of trinkets, but he pulled on his shoes and dutifully followed his silent father across the yard and up the stairs to his apartment.

They were all the way into the living room before Keith spoke, refusing to meet his gaze. "I don't think it's right."

For a moment Clay couldn't think what the heck his dad was talking about, and even once it clicked he was confused. "You mean me and Maggie?"

His father glanced up quickly, then away, but not before Clay had seen the disdain in his expression. "Her husband's barely gone, and she's already going out on the town with another man?" Keith shook his head. "I'm not one who likes to judge, but I'm damned disappointed. In both of you."

Sudden shocking pain gripped Clay, like icy fingers clutched around his heart. Of all the things he'd never expected to hear from his father... "I thought you knew. We've been seeing each other for weeks. It's not—"

"First I've seen of it. You're a grown man, Clay, and you make your own decisions, but I think you moved too fast. It's like spitting on your friend's grave." Keith walked to the far side of the room, shaking his head. "I can't believe you'd be involved in something so dishonouring to a good man's memory."

A blast of heat finally loosened his tongue, yet it was

respect for the past that kept Clay from lashing out at his father. Respect for the pain Keith had gone through losing his wife, and how much it had impacted him for so many years.

That's why instead of telling his dad to take a flying leap, Clay spoke softly, hoping to find a small point of reason they could connect on. It wasn't as if he hadn't worked through his own guilt regarding this. "Cameron *was* a good man, Dad. A great husband to Maggie and a great friend to me, but us being together is in no way dishonouring to him."

"That's not how I see it." Keith waved a hand at his son, twisting toward the back of the room. "God, I can't even look at you right now. You need to think long and hard about what you're doing, and when you come to your senses, then we can talk."

An ultimatum? Fuck that. Clay couldn't help snapping back. "Or what? What if we *don't* come to our senses?"

Keith cleared his throat, one hand on the doorframe to his bedroom. His back to Clay. "If that's your decision, then so be it. I have to work with you, but nothing more. Don't you come around to any family gathering with her, or bring her by here. I don't want to see the two of you together."

For fucks sake. "Really, Dad? You're that set against us just because—"

Keith Thompson shut the door firmly, cutting off the conversation.

It took half a dozen deep breaths for Clay to regain his control. He stood there in the middle of the dark room, fists clenched, driven to rush forward and have this out with the foolish old man. Staying put because it was his *father* being an asshole, and the man had been forced to the edge of hell and come back broken.

Clay hated what he'd heard from his father's lips, but he knew when the festering pain had been planted. Even thirty years later Keith Thompson was as in love with his wife as the day he proposed, and having her torn away twelve years ago had changed him.

Changed them all—Clay down to Katy.

This wasn't the end of the discussion, not by a long shot, but for today he would let it ride.

He took the stairs slowly, pulling himself together before walking back in the door at Gage and Katy's. And if his smile was a little brittle around the edges, no one seemed to notice.

CHAPTER 14

Something was wrong.

The evening had started wonderfully, and she'd enjoyed being around the family. The Thompson clan had always been entertaining, ever since she'd walked back into their presence last summer, but now that she'd gotten to know them as individuals, it was even better.

But tonight wasn't like other nights.

Too many things were slightly off. Like how Clay didn't think Troy was seeing anyone, but his brother's gaze kept darting around the room as if he was missing someone. Plus, Troy kept checking his phone for messages, and he'd briefly lit up when one came through.

Then storm clouds had rolled over his expression only a moment later.

After dinner Gage had disappeared to convince a cranky Tanner to sleep, and Katy immediately curled up on the couch, leaning back and listening to the conversation without adding much to it, which was not like her. Not the Katy Maggie knew.

But it was Clay who had done the most complete one-hundred-eighty-degrees turn between dinner and returning from his father's place. He was tense, and his laughter seemed forced. He didn't say anything to his family, so she held her questions until they were back in his truck and headed home.

"Is your dad okay?" The only thing she could think that would affect him this hard was worry.

His grip on the steering wheel tightened. "He's fine. Like he said, he's tired."

Maggie curled her fingers around Clay's biceps and leaned her head against his shoulder, breathing out slowly. "He's lucky he's got such a wonderful family who cares about him."

If anything Clay stiffened more, but he didn't answer her.

Now she knew something was up. Clay always stood up for his family. Always had something good to say about them, even if it was in an "I'm going to kill them for this" kind of way.

They sat in silence for another moment before she tried again. "If something is wrong, let me know. I'm there for you if you need someone to talk to." She squeezed his arm and allowed a soft chuckle to escape. "Its only fair—you listen to me all the time. I owe you one, or a hundred."

Clay pressed his lips to the top of her head like a silent benediction. "Thank you, but it's nothing. I guess it was a longer day than I thought. I'm out of practice shopping with the ladies."

A yawn escaped her. "You and me both."

He was still tense. Whatever had upset him, he wasn't willing to share and she wasn't going to push. Not yet. They had a ways to go in this relationship, figuring out what came next. Even though she craved the intimacy of sharing concerns, she hoped in time it would come.

"Thank you for the wonderful day," Maggie said softly as he pulled into her driveway.

"No problem. I enjoyed it too."

He walked her to the door and stood at her side as she worked the deadbolt. "Did you want to come in?" she asked.

Clay hesitated, and the brief pause became longer and longer until the silence was nearly painful before he spoke. "I need to go home tonight."

The unspoken words *I have a lot on my mind* drifted between them. So Maggie kissed him good night, a nearly chaste caress, then stepped into her house, and closed and locked the door behind her.

She watched him plod back to the truck, hands jammed into his pockets, his head bent forward, shoulders curled as if he were in pain. She wanted to run outside and wrap herself around him. Demand that he let her in and tell her what was wrong.

What she did instead was wait until he backed out of the driveway and his truck disappeared down the road. As she stood there, deafening silence snuck out from the darkest corners and crumpled her defenses. Maggie gritted her teeth as she wandered through the house and turned on music, filling the rooms with white noise because she couldn't bear how very alone she felt.

AFTER THAT NIGHT at the Thompson birthday party, though, Clay rallied. He never spoke about what had gone wrong, and she didn't poke, and slowly they moved on. Whatever it was that had bothered him didn't intrude very often, and having his very keen attention firmly on her the rest of the time definitely gave her a warm glow inside.

So much had changed in such a short time—that seemed to be the theme of her life this past year. May was nearly over, and Maggie faced most days with a fair bit of optimism.

The weather warmed enough construction progressed quickly at the Habitat site, and after work she took trips to watch as the row of four single-story attached houses began to grow in place like some kind of wood-and-mortar flowers.

She stayed out of the construction team's way best she could, using her rake and trowel to break up the soil and prepare it for when she could begin landscaping.

Working on the project gave her a chance to mindlessly use her hands while pondering what to do next in her life. Not just with her job, but things like home renovations, and if she should upgrade her car, and all the decisions she had to make on her own. After doing everything with another person for so long, it was strange to be in complete control. She was sure she was going to screw up royally at least a few times.

Her phone rang, and she paused to answer it. "Hey, you."

"Hey, gorgeous. You out at the project already?" Clay asked.

"For about fifteen minutes. Are you able to make it today?"

"Yup, just leaving the shop. If I walk, will you give me a ride home?"

Maggie stretched her back and examined the sturdy walls of the apartments in front of her. "Is that code for 'Can I come over for supper?'"

He chuckled. "I'm surprised you didn't accuse me of plotting a booty call."

"Ha. I can if you want."

"Accuse me, or give me one?"

His tone said he was wearing a dirty grin as he said it, and the fact she could clearly picture his face made her smile as well. "That depends. How soon can you get here? I only booty call with guys I meet before four p.m."

"Hanging up now. I can't sprint with a phone in my hands."

Maggie laughed as she slipped her phone into her pocket and went back to work.

Getting involved with Clay, though? That had been exactly what she'd needed, and she didn't regret a single minute. She didn't care that some of her coworkers thought it was too soon. Everything inside her told her this was right, in spite of the brief dark moments. That he was a good man, and that the way he made her feel couldn't be wrong.

It wasn't just about sex. They talked, and sat together to do mindless tasks, like in the days before she had pushed their relationship ahead, but she sure appreciated that there was something extra between them. She didn't sit beside him on the couch as they watched movies; she cuddled in close as he cradled her. She didn't feel guilty about putting her hand on his thigh, or lifting her lips and asking for a kiss —she'd craved such moments of affection since Cameron had died.

And in bed... Holy. Moly. He knew instinctively how to push her buttons. If anything, the man was still holding back and letting her control the reins, which had to be driving him crazy. It wasn't like Clay to let others call the shots. Not just in sex, but in everything, she'd noticed he liked to take command.

When he and Cameron used to do things together, her husband had always found it entertaining, and frankly, a relief. He had no objections to letting Clay be in charge of decision-making like where they'd go play pool.

Yet now he skirted the edge between being the Clay she knew and someone far too cautious, as if he were afraid that at any moment what they had would pop like a bubble.

She grabbed a rake and dragged it over the soil, dislodging the rubbish and weeds that were trying to gain new ground. Maggie really didn't know exactly where their relationship was going, so she could hardly blame him for being cautious.

This was the point where doubts sank in. What she was doing, what *they* were doing, caused her no doubts.

Thinking about the future?

Until she knew *for sure* what she wanted she didn't feel comfortable pressuring Clay, and the whole idea of forever was currently hidden behind a thick fog. So she did the only thing she could, using the advice everyone kept giving her.

One day at a time. Keep moving forward.

She'd just pulled off her gloves and dropped to her knees to open a garbage bag when something crashed into the brick wall above her. Glass shattered into a million pieces and rained down on her head, a sharp pain striking her cheek. She twisted her head away, raising her hands to protect herself. A second and third bottle followed, the sound of youthful catcalls loud on the air, and she froze as glimmers of light appeared on the back of her hands, shards of glass embedded in her skin.

Shock kept her in place. Should she stand up and make sure they knew she was there? Or would that be more dangerous?

The vandals tossed more bottles farther down the wall,

and she chose to remain hidden, sure it was just bad luck she'd been caught in their line of fire. The sound of squealing tires faded into the distance, and she let out a shaky breath, confident she was out of danger.

Maggie glanced down at the soil, sadness slipping in at the work she'd have to redo even as she considered how she was going to pull her phone from her pocket.

The vandalism wasn't bad, but she was shaking enough she wasn't going to drive herself home. And the glass...

Then Clay was there, bursting out of nowhere to crouch beside her, his big hands gentle on her shoulders as he brought her to her feet. "Damn kids," he swore. "I saw them taking off as I arrived." He glanced over her rapidly, concern in his eyes as he lifted a hand to carefully touch her throbbing cheek. "Shit. You're bleeding."

"I'm okay. It's just a few cuts." She shook her head and glass tumbled down her arms. "Drat. I don't want to move. I have glass everywhere."

Clay was already removing pieces from her hair, dropping the larger chunks into the metal garbage can beside them. "I'll get these out then we can take you to the hospital—"

"I don't need a hospital," she snapped as too many memories rushed her. *No.* No hospitals.

"You're bleeding," he repeated in a dangerous tone.

"Just a little. I don't need a hospital," she insisted, her heart rate pounding faster than it had when the vandalism occurred. "You...*you* can take care of me."

The expression on his face as he caught a closer glimpse of her bloody hands was soul curdling—she'd seen that look before on her husband's face when she'd gotten hurt. Classic masculine protectiveness combined with helpless agitation at not being able to take away her pain.

Her frustrations and fears faded as the urge to reassure Clay rose. "I'm okay, honest."

"We need to get you home," he growled.

This wasn't the time to try to calm him down. "I should call Daniel and let them know what happened," she murmured.

"Later." It wasn't a suggestion.

Nope. She definitely wasn't going to fight with him when he was in this mood. So she didn't say anything about getting her phone out of her pocket, and she didn't comment how she hoped the kids who were upset would get over it soon. She would hate for the trouble to continue after the seniors had moved in—frightening them would be a terrible thing.

It wasn't until Clay hustled her into his house that she realized she should have specified *which* home she'd meant. He took her straight to the bathroom, grabbed tweezers and went to work removing the glass from her hands. Her wedding ring a spot of shining gold against a field of red scratches.

When she winced at an especially deep one, he got that much quieter.

Maggie didn't protest when he went to take off her clothes.

Well, she complained a little. "Can we do this somewhere we can pick up the glass easier if there's any stuck in my clothing?"

A shudder rocked him, but he took her into the kitchen and threw a sheet on the floor for her to stand on. "Are you *sure* you're okay?"

She lifted her chin and looked him straight in the eyes as she nodded. "Clay, I'm fine."

He helped her out of her T-shirt, both of them moving

like molasses when he discovered a sprinkling of shards stuck to her skin. He reached for the button on her jeans and pulled them down, leaving her clad in nothing but her panties...and her work boots and socks. The image struck her as enormously funny, and a snort escaped her. And then tension made her snicker, and by the time Clay looked up from where he'd bent to undo her laces, she was full-out giggling.

He shook his head, an incredulous expression on his face. "What about this could possibly make you laugh?"

She plopped her hands on her hips and twisted into a pose. "Fashion model of the year, Maggie Ward, demonstrating the finest in gardening styles."

His lips twitched, but she didn't *quite* get a smile out of him.

She dropped a hand to his head and cautiously ran her fingers over his hair. "You need to take a deep breath, Clay, and let it out slowly. Nothing happened. It was some kids with an attitude, and I was in the wrong place at the wrong time, and I need a shower. That's *all*."

He laid his head against her belly and took a few of those deep breaths she'd suggested. She held on to him, stroking her fingers over his shoulders, waiting for him to be ready to move on.

"I need to take care of you," he whispered

She caught hold of a few strands of his hair and tugged so he would look up at her. "I have no problem with that," she teased. "Honest. As long as you understand that I like to take care of you as well."

He rose to his feet then helped her shake her hair carefully over the sheet, small shards of glass falling like slivers of sunlight. It seemed to take forever, and she was glad for his helping arm when he finally guided her to the bathroom and into the walk-in shower.

Maggie expected he would leave her and let her shower alone, but it seemed his idea of *taking care of her* was a little more hands-on than that. She watched through the open shower door as he stripped down to nothing but muscles and a serious expression.

A quiver of something suspiciously familiar hit her in the chest. She didn't want to analyze it, or poke at it, she just wanted to let it roll over her and take her under. So she opened her arms and welcomed him in.

Let him take care of her with soap and caresses and careful, careful kisses that said more to her than any bull-horn-blared declaration could.

And all the while the faint whisper inside kept swelling in volume until there was no way to deny it.

She was falling in love.

She knew this road well, and had traveled it before. It was a *good* road, one with amazing side excursions and beautiful views to enjoy. Yet she clutched her secret inside, not willing to share it. Not even with him, it was so fresh and new and tender.

But sometime soon...

HE'D BEEN LIVING in hell. The past couple weeks had been tearing him in two as he tried to balance caring for Maggie and taking care of his family which included his stubborn, disapproving father.

Clay brushed the palms of his hands over her skin, keeping her close even as he ranted at himself for not being there when she really needed him. Maggie leaned against him, covering his hands with hers to guide them over her body. She wasn't shy about what she wanted, but he moved only as fast as he felt safe. Turning her carefully under the warm shower as the bubbles swirled down the drain by their feet.

"Do you want to go to the police?" he asked.

She reacted instantly. Spinning to face him, her eyes wide with shock. "Of course not. They were kids acting stupid, and I don't even know for sure who it was."

Clay could do some digging and find out whose car he'd seen vanishing like a spooked rabbit. He brushed his thumb over her cheek where a red stripe marred her skin. "They were stupid kids who were trespassing and vandalizing, and they *hurt* you."

"It's a scratch. I've gotten worse trimming rosebushes without wearing my gloves."

She wasn't going to give in so he pretended to give up, carefully running his fingers over the marks and cuts on the back of her hands. "I have some cream to put on these, and a couple of them need bandages."

"Fine. I have something else I need you to do for me first, though."

Then damn if she didn't lean back on the tile wall and run her hands up her body until she was cupping her breasts.

Being near her always made him hard, but he'd been so worried that he'd managed to put aside his ever-present desire while he made sure all the glass was gone. But with her staring at him, a low moan of pleasure escaping her lips as she touched herself—

His cock rose like a barometer. He shoved aside his fears and tried to fake lighthearted. "Let me guess. You want me to move a delivery at the greenhouse."

Maggie laughed, then tilted her head until she was peeking flirtatiously at him from under her lashes. "*Clay...*"

"Oh, right, this is a booty call."

He gave an exaggerated sigh then moved in on her wiggling body, trapping her with an arm on either side of her head as he covered her lips with his and kissed her senseless. Partly frustration, partly fear—all of it came out as he took her lips and possessed her.

She caught her arms around his shoulders, moving against him enticingly as he shoved a hand between them, skimming over her belly until he could cup her sex. Maggie rocked her hips as a low whimper escaped her and a shock wave slammed into him.

What the fuck was *wrong* with him?

He jerked his lips from hers and rested his head on the tiles, fighting to cool himself down before he ravished her instead of taking care of her like he'd promised.

"Oh, God. Don't stop," Maggie whispered, digging her nails into his shoulders and scratching him.

Clay fell to his knees, pinning her to the wall with an arm across her hips as he stroked a finger through her curls. "Not going to stop until you beg me to."

He put his mouth to her sex and licked the full length, settling for a brief flick at her clit this first round. He was rewarded with a full-body shudder as Maggie dropped her hands to his head and held on tight.

He wasn't going anywhere. Slow and deliberate, he licked over and over, slipping a finger into her sex as he used his teeth and lips on the small peak of her clit. Sucking it with a gentle pulse that she echoed with her hips. He tightened his grip to keep her in place, easing a second finger to join the first as he sped up his tongue. Flicking rapidly against the tiny nub as he stroked his fingers inside, reaching for the most sensitive spots.

"Clay. Oh, *yes...*"

She inched her legs apart as if trying to give him even more room. He wanted so much more, but the sounds slipping from her lips along with his name were like a drug pumping through his veins. His cock was so hard, his balls tight against his body. He ignored all of that and focused on her, driving her wild until her grip tightened and her muscles tensed. Her pussy squeezed tight around his fingers as a purr of satisfaction rolled down on top of him.

He had her out of the shower and wrapped in an enormous towel before her breathing was back to normal. Which was fine by him because he wasn't done. Clay placed her on his bed like he was lowering precious china.

She caught hold before he could move away, her warm palms pressed to his cheeks as she stared at him with a teasing smile. "I'm not going to break. Really."

Clay crawled over her then rolled so she was on top, her hands pressed to his chest. Their legs tangled together, the heavy shaft of his erection pressed against her soft belly. "Never said you were. Now get up here," he ordered.

Confusion blurred her eyes for a moment until he caught her by the hips and began moving her forward to where he wanted her.

She hesitated. "Umm..."

Oh, this was sweet. "Maggie Ward, is that a blush I see on your cheeks?"

"Maybe," she muttered. "Really? You want me to...sit on your face?"

She sounded scandalized, but also intrigued. Clay lifted her closer, positioning her in spite of her mild protests. "It's just a different position, Mags, that's all."

With both hands gripping the headboard, and her knees on either side of his head, she tilted her head toward him and offered another adorable peek at her flushed face. "It's a very *intimate*— Oh my God, *Clay*..."

If she wanted to keep complaining, that was her choice. He had something else to focus on. Her sweet pussy was right there in front of him, slick with moisture, her clit begging for more attention.

It was far easier to reach her most sensitive spots from this angle. Laving his tongue up one side then down the other. Circling her clit before stabbing deep and fucking her with his tongue. The headboard creaked softly as Maggie rocked against his face.

This time when she called out he didn't stop. He kept playing and teasing, not ready to give up the sweetness of having her at his complete mercy.

"Stop. Stop, oh my God, stop before I collapse," she said with a laugh, wiggling from side to side on the bed until he let her go.

Clay curled up to a sitting position and wiped his mouth, a cocky grin breaking free. "Told you you'd beg for me to stop."

Mischief danced in her eyes, and she pivoted on the mattress and crawled toward him. "Let me return the favour."

Hell, no. "You put your lips anywhere near my cock and I'll go off like a rocket."

"I want to," she insisted.

Her fingers wrapped around his length, and he braced himself. He was seconds away from spilling already. But more than that, the sight of the scratches and cuts on her hands and arms sent a flurry of emotion through him that was impossible to withstand.

He got out of her clutches and pulled her back to the mattress, pinning her in place with his body as he took her lips again. Careful, but thorough until she stopped protesting and went soft and willing under him. Her nails marked his back all the way to his ass as she scratched lightly.

Clay spoke against her lips when they paused for air. "Some other time you can blow me, but right now I want to touch you everywhere."

"It's really hard to grumble when you're so damn attentive," Maggie complained. "Okay, fine. Have your way with me. Turn me into a bowl of jelly."

If that was a challenge, it was one he was more than willing to accept. He worshiped her breasts, licking her nipples while he played with the soft curves. Teasing with his teeth, and sucking lightly until she rocked against him. He pressed one leg more firmly between her thighs to give her something to press against, but he knew from the needy noises she was making it wasn't enough.

He couldn't decide what he wanted more—to drop back between her legs again where the sweetest taste in the world lay, or slide up and kiss her lips because *that* was even better.

And then there was no holding back because he was going to explode if he didn't get inside her. He grabbed a condom and rolled it on, returning between her thighs as quickly as possible

Maggie caught his face in her hands, her eyes so bright and clear as he eased the head of his cock between her smooth folds.

"Its like slipping into heaven," he said. "So fucking good."

She nodded her agreement, her lips drawn into an O of

pleasure as he pulled back until just the tip of his cock clung to her opening.

"More," she whispered, stroking her fingers over his cheeks as she stared into his eyes.

"Yes, more," he agreed. "Like this?"

He pushed all the way in, as deep as he could, and held himself motionless.

Maggie squirmed, trying to get even closer. "Tease."

He was driving himself mad as well. Another slow withdrawal, another deep plunge, again and again until a sharp tingling at the base of his spine warned him he had only seconds left.

Clay gritted his teeth and adjusted position so he could put his fingers to her clit.

She gasped for air. "Oh, Clay, I can't."

"Again," he demanded. "However long it takes."

He rocked them together steadily, adjusting position, changing his touch until he saw the biggest reaction. The place where his body kept Maggie careening toward pleasure.

It was a good thing she came when she did because he was about to break. The sound of her satisfied exhale was like a trigger, and he didn't even finish his thrust. Just came, spurting into the condom so hard he thought he might've blown it apart.

He withdrew quickly, yet kept his arms around her, his lips coming to meet with hers. He wasn't going to leave her, not even for the moment he desperately needed to get rid of the condom.

Maggie's lashes fluttered open, and she let out a deep, satisfied sigh. "I know this is totally unromantic, but I want to sleep here tonight, so maybe you should take care of things before we have to fight for who *doesn't* get stuck with the wet spot?"

Clay planted one last kiss on her lips before rolling away and following instructions. "I have extra sheets," he teased.

She adjusted position on the bed, throwing back the covers and moving the pillows to where she wanted them as she settled in. "If you want to remake the bed, go for it. I'm done with chores for the day."

"Which means I'm taking you out for dinner?" Clay asked as he crawled back into bed and pulled her into his arms.

Maggie rested her head on his chest, drawing designs on his abdomen with her fingertips. "Oh, I don't mind cooking," she said. "It's anything to do with laundry that can kiss my ass."

They lay together, warm and comfortable, and Clay wondered at how things had changed in the last couple hours. He'd gone from complete frustration with his situation to gut-clenching fear to such bone-deep satisfaction...

...and suddenly everything fell into place.

He didn't know how to deal with the unreasonable demand his father had laid on him. He still didn't know where this was going, this thing between him and Maggie. All he knew for sure was this is where she belonged, *in his arms*, and that was the only thing that ultimately mattered.

The one thing he would not give up was *her*.

CHAPTER 15

Clay watched the clock, timing the break in his task as close to three o'clock as possible.

"I've gotta go in a minute," he told Gage. "I'll finish the rest of the job tonight."

His friend glanced up from the engine, concern on his face. "Anything you need help with?"

Clay shook his head and kept his mouth shut. The last thing he wanted was for someone to try to talk him out of his plan.

"You guys done Johnson's car yet?" His dad, shouting from the door of the front lobby where he'd been spending more and more time camped out. He refused to come into the workshop unless it was vital, and didn't *that* make Clay feel like a shit.

Gage shouted back. "Keys are on the rack. It's been done since noon." He turned back to his friend and lifted a brow. "What the hell is going on with him?"

His brother Len was paying attention from the next car over. "Dad's got his knickers in a knot over something, and he's glaring at Clay when he thinks no one is looking. What did you do to him, bro?"

It was so tempting to spill the beans. Get it out in the open and yet...

He couldn't. It would be like pushing his father under a bus. Keith was wrong—full-out *wrong* to be so judgmental—but after spending years keeping his family together, Clay couldn't do it. There had to be a way to remove the spike that'd been driven between them without sacrificing family.

But no way in hell would he give up his time with Maggie, either.

He dragged a hand through his hair, and the time on the digital clock clicked over like an hourglass running low on sand. "Whatever it is, he'll figure it out. I really need to go."

Gage and Len exchanged glances. Len, of course, wouldn't say anything. Gage—his expression promised he'd bring this up as soon as he could. And maybe by then Clay would be ready to talk about it, but right now he had a little fire and brimstone to administer.

He pulled into the parking lot outside the Boys and Girls Club just as the school bell buzzed in the distance.

A blast of memories hit.

That sound had signaled the end of his relaxing and the start of another round of unending labour. Hurrying home from school and going straight to the shop to discover what his dad had accomplished since they'd left him that morning.

Some days were better than others. The good days Keith kept out of the bottle and worked on the jobs that were too technical for Clay and Mitch to figure out. The bad days...? He'd dreaded the ones where he'd find his father slumped in the back room with not much more accomplished than the empty bottle on the desk.

It'd taken years to move forward from that hell, but they'd done it. Clay and Mitch had kept the garage from going under, while Len babysat the youngest two and helped however he could. They'd done it as a family, waiting until the time Keith dragged himself out from under the liquor and straightened up his act.

There hadn't been a lot to celebrate those first couple of years, and then everything changed for the better. Slowly, never completely going back to how it was, but in some ways, they'd been knit together even stronger than before.

So no matter how much he wanted to tell Keith to shove it, he didn't know if he was capable. He didn't know if he was strong enough to untangle himself from the fire-forged cords that tied him to his family.

A trickle of kids wandered across from the school fields toward the old clubhouse building. Voices came from around the back basketball court, but he focused his attention on the main doors.

Maggie had talked to Daniel, and in the end they'd agreed not to track down the kids and press charges. Didn't mean Clay couldn't scare the little shits into minding their manners.

On the other side of the doors, he discovered loud laughter and rambunctious activity. A large gathering of kids crowded the front of the room, and Clay headed toward them, faltering to a stop as a decidedly familiar female voice rang over the chaos.

"Stand back and then *everyone* will be able to see."

Maggie held the attention of the good two-dozen kids aged eight to sixteen. The table in front of her was covered with seedling trays, a mess of seed packages piled to one side and more trays stacked beside that.

She looked around the room, obviously continuing

whatever lecture she'd been giving. "So now that I showed you what I've got growing, it's your turn. I brought enough everyone can plant two trays. One you can use anywhere you want—at your house, in one of the community garden boxes. Outside the center."

"Where does the other one go?" The question came from one of the Mason kids, a single dad who worked at the fire station. Josh was hanging on the table, nearly tipping it with his weight as he attempted to peek into the trays.

"I'm going to use the rest of the plants to make the new Habitat for Humanity houses pretty." She lifted her hand to stop the chorus of groans that echoed around the room. "Really? You don't think that's a good thing to do with them?"

"But they're *old*," Josh's twin sister complained.

"Yup," Maggie said with a nod, a smile on her face as she pulled a package of seeds from the pile and offered it to Jenny. "That's what happens when you live for a long time."

Some of the older kids snickered, but nobody interrupted.

"I think they're very happy to have a new place to move into soon, but did you know some of them have lived in the same house for almost their entire lives? That might make them sad to leave, so it would be really nice to have the new place looking pretty for them. I know it would mean a lot to them if you guys were involved with making that happen."

The more wiggly kids were crowding forward, but for the most part Maggie worked them like she was some kind of snake charmer. With a clap of her hands she paired up older kids with younger ones, sending the two biggest boys to get an oversized bag of potting soil out of the trunk of her car.

Clay stood at the side of the room bemused, feeling as if

he'd been schooled along with the rest of them. It wasn't the fire and brimstone he'd intended on preaching. It was a hell of a lot more subtle, and a hell of a lot more effective, from what he could tell.

Her gaze fell on him, and a rosy glow covered her cheeks. He paced forward and was rewarded with a welcoming smile.

"Good. Another volunteer."

"At your service." He was. Totally and completely. "*Anything* you need."

Maggie caught his innuendo. "Behave," she muttered, but she was smiling.

For the next fifteen minutes, the room turned into a miniature greenhouse as dirty fingers picked up seeds and pressed them into warm soil. Clay wasn't sure how well some of the seeds were going to grow. They'd been pushed into the soil and pulled out then pushed back in.

He caught one inventive young man pouring an entire seed packet into the same hole, but he took his cue from Maggie and didn't say anything. Just smiled at him then later felt as if he'd done something miraculous when he caught Maggie's approving gaze focused on him over the children's heads.

It took a third of the time he thought it would before Maggie was putting the last of the name labels on the trays and guiding the kids toward the outside doors.

"Since you don't have enough windows in the clubhouse, I'll take the trays back to my greenhouse to help them grow." She tweaked Josh's nose with a smile. "I'll water them, but anytime you want to stop in after school to see how they're doing, you know where to find me."

"When will we plant them?"

Clay spoke up, softly but kept his words firm. "That

depends. We need to get the buildings in place first, but we can't get them done if the site keeps getting vandalized."

Maggie held her breath. Clay wanted to reassure her he *was* following her lead, only the older kids especially needed to know there was a line that couldn't be crossed anymore.

"If everything goes well from now on, the plants should be ready right before school gets out." She smiled sympathetically at the grumbles her announcement received.

That had to seem like forever, especially to the littlest kids. Clay pushed aside the rest of his need for vengeance as his protective instincts veered toward new targets. "In the meantime, I noticed there's a basketball hoop outside. Anyone want to shoot a few?"

He got a loud cheer as a rush of bodies fled into the afternoon sunshine. Clay held back as the kids left, and he ended up alone with Maggie for a moment, basking in the sunshine of her smile.

"You old softy," she murmured before pulling him down so she could press a kiss to his lips.

She hadn't needed protecting today. The idea was going to take some time to sink in. "I wasn't about to rain on your parade. You're pretty amazing."

She pushed him toward the door. "I am. And I'm real good at basketball. Get ready to get your butt kicked."

HE WAS STILL HOLDING BACK.

Maggie got ready for a night out dancing at Traders, pulling on a new dress, one that had made Clay's eyes light up when he'd seen her try it on. She slipped into the bathroom to do something a little fancier with her hair than simply pulling it back into a ponytail.

She put on touch of makeup as she considered why the secret he was keeping made her feel so uncomfortable. It wasn't that she expected him to spill the beans just because she wanted him to.

It was subtler than that. Heck, she was keeping a secret from him, and maybe...

She planted both hands on the bathroom counter and leaned forward to blow a raspberry at herself before offering her reflection a stern scold. "There you go, falling in love with another man who thinks he always knows what's best for you."

It had taken a while for her to convince Cameron that he didn't need to protect her all the time. Looked as if she was going to have to teach that same lesson to another hard-headed sweetheart of a man. She was in love, and as much as Clay took care of her and everyone around him, she wanted to be able to give back as well.

And *that* was why she wanted to know what was poking him. So she could help him, and they could get through it together.

He picked her up at the front door and kissed her long and deep before they strolled out to his truck.

"Hmm, I like how the evening is starting," Maggie said with a smile.

Clay let his gaze linger on her legs. "Me too."

She slipped her fingers into his and held on tight, letting him lead her into the noise and warmth of the pub. He took her in through the family side, the section with dartboards and pool tables and lots of seating in long rows. A number of large gatherings were talking loudly and animatedly around shared pitchers and plates of food.

"Is your family coming out tonight?" she asked, raising her voice above the crowd.

"Mitch and Anna, for sure," he said, waving toward the corner of the room where familiar faces turned and waved back. "They'll probably spend some time with the Colemans, but—"

He jerked to a stop and she bumped into his side, catching his arm to keep her balance. Clay instantly turned her in a new direction, guiding her the long way around to where the door to the dance floor stood.

She glanced over her shoulder to see what was wrong, but nothing caught her attention. "What was that all about?"

The volume only increased as they stepped through the opening to the second half of Traders. Clay leaned his lips close by her ear as they paused to let their eyes adjust to the dimmer lighting. "I just wanted to get over here before the dance floor got full."

Okaaaay.

Boy, was he a shitty liar.

Still, she let it go. Keeping tight hold of his arm as he led her through the crowd and onto the hardwood floor in front of the band. And then it wasn't awkward because she was in his arms and that was exactly where she wanted to be. She slipped her fingers around his neck as he settled his hands on her hips and gazed down at her.

"There we go," she teased. "You do know how to smile after all."

"Stop it," he grumbled.

She arched a brow at him. "I'll have you know you're on my naughty list."

"Is that supposed to be a *bad* thing?"

Maggie laughed. "Okay, let me rephrase. You said you would—"

He twirled her so quickly she lost track of what she was going to say, confusion rising as he guided them across the dance floor way quicker than the beat of the music called for.

When they finally settled on the opposite side of the room, Maggie planted her hands on his chest and pushed back until there was open space between them. "What was that about?"

Was that guilt drifting across his face? She glanced around the room, determined to find what was going on to make him act so irrational.

It wasn't that difficult to find a group of locals with their heads bent together, casting numerous glances in their direction.

"Oh, for fucks sake," Maggie complained.

Clay tilted her head back, his fingers under her chin. "Ignore them. They're idiots."

She pulled herself from his grasp. "I'm not talking about them, I'm talking about *you*. Are you still trying to protect me?"

His jaw fell open before he slammed his lips together.

Yup, that's what she'd figured. She folded her arms across her chest and gave him a dirty look. "I thought we talked about this. I thought we talked about this a long time ago."

"I don't want you to be hurt."

Big, kindhearted buffoon.

He was right, though. Maggie had had enough of the gossip...in her own way. Fuck this, if they were going to be talking, why not talk about something with a little *zing* value? She slipped back into his arms, locked her fingers behind his neck and tugged Clay toward her, bringing their lips together so she could give him a fiery kiss right there in the middle of the dance floor.

It was effective for more than one reason. First, someone in the room let out a sharp wolf whistle, which caused a round of applause to break out, but more importantly, Clay kissed her back. He didn't try to pull away, didn't try to hide them. He gave as good as he got, only letting her free when her legs were trembling.

"Get a room," somebody shouted, the dirty comment greeted by a combination of cheers and hissed disapproval.

Clay stared down at her, far more confusion on his face than she'd expected. "Well. So much for controlling the gossip."

She dipped her chin in approval. "Good. Because what you're supposed to be doing is dancing with me."

"This isn't over yet," he warned.

"Oh, sweetie." Maggie tapped her fingers on his chest and offered her best *you're going to get what's coming to you later* smile. "That's my line."

CHAPTER 16

She kept them on the dance floor for two solid hours, barely pausing to have a cold drink before hauling them back out. Clay let her boss him around, his fascination rising with each passing minute. Yeah, there were people in the room watching with disapproval in their eyes, but she sure didn't see them.

Instead she looked up at him with her emotions right there and readable like an open book. How much she cared for him, and wanted him, and a tiny hint of exasperation, as if she were pissed.

"Stop looking around the room like you want to make heads roll," Maggie ordered as they slowed their pace for the next song. "I'm not going to break because of a few snotty comments."

No, she obviously wasn't, and Clay tried hard to pull his caveman tendencies back under control, but it was damn impossible to hold back completely. He settled for shooting warning glares at the worst offenders.

By the time she seemed ready to call it a night, a layer of pleasure floated over a bed of banked coals. Something needed to change, and soon, but he wasn't sure what. The people at Traders? He could mostly ignore.

His father was a far bigger dilemma.

"My place," Maggie ordered as she pressed a brief kiss to his lips then tugged him out of the pub.

Clay didn't protest. Just took her home and followed her into the living room, watching with amusement as she darted around the living room and dining areas, closing the curtains tightly. "Let me guess. You're planning on killing me, and you don't want any witnesses?"

"Don't give me any ideas," she said softly.

She met him in the middle of the room, her head tilted to the side as if she was thinking hard. As if she knew what she had to say but wasn't sure *how* to say it. "Tell me the truth. Does it bother you that we're together? Do you think it's wrong, or that we should have waited longer?"

Clay shook his head. "God, Maggie, *no*. That's not it at all."

"Then I don't get it. Why is it such a big deal to you that other people have a problem with it? Other people do a lot of things differently than we would, and when we disapprove they don't turn around and try to live their lives by our rules."

He caught her hands in his, trapped by loyalty and far too much history. "It's not that simple."

"It's not, and yet it is. Taking care of me is one thing, and I know, damn, those early days after Cameron died, you helped hold me together. Back then what I needed was a big, strong protector, and that's what you gave me, and I'm *so* glad."

"But you don't need me the same way?" The words came out brittle. What if she decided he was too much bullshit to put up with and it was time to end them? His heart pounded as if he'd been running a marathon.

Her expression softened. "You're right, I don't need you the same way."

Fuck.

She hurried to finish. "Don't look at me like that. What I'm trying to say is I need you *more*. And I need more *from* you, and I want to know—is that what you want too?"

"More of you?"

She nodded. "I don't really need a protector, what I need is a partner. Someone who wants me beside them because we're equals. Because together, we're more than we are apart."

The ice that encased him vanished, and he could breathe. It hadn't registered exactly how far into his heart she'd managed to wiggle.

The truth burst out. "I can't promise to stop protecting you."

Maggie rolled her eyes before settling into a tolerant grin. "Look, I'm not going to object to you going caveman on me *sometimes*, but I'm not as fragile as I was a couple months ago. I don't want you to feel like you have to be so... careful with me all the time."

He caught the innuendo. "Is this about sex?"

A burst of laughter escaped. "Partly? But it's also about *everything*. I'm not going to shrivel up because somebody at Traders gives me a dirty look for holding your hand. The only way other people are going to get over whatever issues they have— No, forget that." She got right in his face and glared at him intently. "Us being together, this is a *good* thing, agreed?"

He nodded.

Maggie swallowed hard. "Then... Let's be together.

However we want and in whatever way that works for us. Sharing what makes us happy *and* what's hurting us."

Fuck. He knew exactly what she was hinting at.

He wanted to be a partner with her, God did he ever want to be completely and wholly together. And it didn't matter what his father thought, because this was going to happen. Only...

If he shared what was bothering him, Maggie would forever carry that awful memory. Even if Clay knocked sense into his father, having that ugly judgment come out into the open could never be undone.

And that *wasn't* what he wanted in his relationship with Maggie. It wasn't what he wanted to be a part of his siblings' memories.

So, fuck it all, he agreed with her and yet *still* had to choose to one final time do what he thought was best, no matter how much it might hurt.

He would talk to his father, in private and soon, and then deal with the fallout. He was choosing her.

Choosing *them*.

He caught her close and kissed her as an answer, because it was the best solution he could think of. She smiled against his lips before pulling back and tapping him firmly on the chest. "Stop distracting me. I want an answer. Can you do that? Can you sometimes be lovey-dovey and tender and romantic, and other times..."

"...and other times more energetic?"

Her eyes lit up, and a rosy flush spread over her face, this time not caused by fury. "If you're serious, time to put your money where your mouth is. Or how about you let *me* put my mouth where the hell *I* want."

He wasn't quite sure what she was talking about until she dropped to her knees in front of him. Maggie tilted her head back to flash him a dirty smile as she reached for the button on his jeans.

Clay caught hold of her hands. "No, baby, this isn't—"

She curled her fingertips into his waistband and held on tight. "The next fifteen minutes I'm in charge. You can have the fifteen minutes after that. Got it?"

It seemed this wasn't the moment for *careful*. He released her wrists and placed his hands at his sides. Waiting to see where she would take this.

"You're in charge, and no more holding back," he agreed. "Maybe you should set a timer." The words rumbled from deep in his chest as he pushed aside everything else and focused on this woman who knew how to drive him wild with barely a touch.

He'd been kidding, but Maggie popped up and headed to the kitchen, coming back with the digital one from off the fridge. "Brilliant. Until this goes off, you have to do everything I say, and that means *everything*."

Maybe. "I'll try."

Sheer utter relief washed across her face followed by dirty anticipation. Maggie wasted no time getting back into position, the timer on the desk counting down. She was nearly vibrating as she stroked her fingers up his length to undo the button at his waistband. Slowly slipping down the zipper before tugging his jeans off his hips. She moaned with satisfaction, rubbing her cheek against the thick length of his cock trapped behind his cotton briefs.

A strangled gasp escaped his lips. Drive him wild? She was going to make him hyperventilate and fucking pass out in the first five minutes.

When she reached in and pulled out his cock, his entire body trembled. A first bit of come had escaped, and she lapped at it, her hot tongue and lips getting him wet as all the blood in his body rushed into one location. He was growing lightheaded. The minx showed no mercy as she hummed with delight, slowly licking, slowly surrounding him with her mouth before pulling back with a wicked suction that threatened to make him fall over.

His knees trembled, and he fucking gave up. Watching her, feeling her touch—she might be in charge, but he knew what he wanted to make this moment even better. Clay thrust his fingers into her hair and tightened his grip. A gasp escaped her, but this time instead of pausing he kept going, cradling her head so he could rock his hips forward and drive his cock deeper into the heated pleasure of her mouth.

He watched. Checked to make sure he wasn't going too far, but he didn't hold back as much either. Maggie gripped his thighs, fingertips digging into his skin as she blew his mind.

Fifteen minutes. He should be able to last that long and then turn the evening the direction he wanted, but her time had barely begun and he was already worried about losing the entire shooting match in the next couple of seconds.

He forced them to a stop, breathing heavily as he fought the instinct to let go. Maggie pulled back, sucking hard as she went, separating from him with a loud *pop*.

"Had enough?" she said sweetly.

"Not fucking likely."

She squealed as he scooped her up, shuffling his way out of the living room, kicking his jeans off behind him as he lowered her to the dining room table.

Maggie bit her lower lip as she waggled her brows at him. "Time flies when you're having fun," she teased.

"Screw the timer. Strip," he ordered.

She placed her hands on the bottom of her dress, lifting it over her head willingly. He reached around and undid her bra, pulling the straps off her shoulders and tossing it behind him. One more wiggle and her panties joined the rest of their clothing abandoned on the floor

Maggie placed her hands behind her on the table and arched her torso toward him, her breasts displayed perfectly. "You're still wearing your shirt," she complained.

"So?" Clay leaned closer, leering down her body. "I didn't say anything about leveling the playing field."

He took her lips, possessive and controlling. Using his mouth to guide her back onto the solid oak table. As soon as she was laid out like a banquet, he moved lower, catching one pink peak in his mouth and sucking hard. Slipping his hands up to cup and caress her breasts as he alternated between her nipples.

And when he put his teeth to the tip, Maggie all but levitated off the table, her fingernails digging into his scalp as he continued to torment her.

He couldn't stop touching her. One hand dropped to between her legs, his fingers slipping between her curls to find she was already wet for him.

"So sweet. I fucking *love* your pussy. I love the way you squeeze around my fingers. The way you clamp so tight around my cock, like you don't ever want to let go."

"*Clay.*" Her voice trembled as he slipped two fingers into her and placed his thumb over her clit, moving quicker and quicker as she writhed under him. Fucking her with his fingers as he went back and wrapped his lips around one nipple.

"Shall I fuck you on the table?" he asked, lips brushing the hard little peak. "I could flip you onto your stomach and drive my cock into you from behind. Or maybe we'll stay right here in this position, with your feet over my shoulders so that when I'm pounding into you, you're bent in two and can't move. No way to escape until I drag every last fucking second of pleasure from you."

Her hips slammed against his hand, and her wavering cry floated across the room.

Careful Clay would've stopped, slowing down to make sure he wasn't pushing her too far. The Clay she claimed she wanted kept going, demanding more. Still holding back from taking everything he wanted, but only because when he finally gave in, it was going to be mind-blowing.

SHE WAS WRUNG out like a dishcloth and he wasn't done with her, and the only thought in her head was a loud *Ye-fucking-ha.*

This was what she'd been looking for the past few weeks. *This* was what had been missing. As Clay pulled his hand from her body and licked his fingers clean, an absolutely filthy smile in his eyes, Maggie wanted to get up on the table and do a victory dance.

Only she couldn't because he'd dropped to his knees, jerked her hips to the edge of the table and put his mouth against her sex.

Some noises escaped her. She didn't think it was a complete sentence. Heck, not even a real word, more like a plea for him to never, ever stop. He jammed his hands under her ass and lifted her tighter to his mouth. Fucking his tongue as deep as he could then coming back and teasing her clit until she wrapped her legs around his head in an attempt to break away.

The only thing that stopped him was her orgasm, her body rocking so hard the table under her jolted and scraped over the floor.

She got a ten-second reprieve as he tore his shirt over his head, jerking it forward hard enough seams ripped. Then she was in the air, clutching his muscular shoulders as he carried her down the hall.

"I'd complain about being hauled around like a sack of grain, but I don't think I can walk," she teased.

She caught a flash of grin in the second before he tossed her on the bed. Literally *tossed*. Maggie stopped herself from rolling, twisting up to a sitting position as he grabbed a condom from the bedside table.

He paused for long enough to roll it down his length, staring at her the entire time. "You're so damn beautiful you make my body ache. I can't fucking believe that I'm here with you. That we're together."

"Believe it," she whispered as he stalked toward her.

He trapped her with his body weight. Kissing her until she was shaking with need. They rolled on the mattress, bodies rubbing together until they ended up sitting on the bed, her straddling his hips, the head of his cock just inside her sex as he pressed his open hands to her bare back. Sealing her breasts to his muscular chest. Their eyes fixed on each other.

He pushed her onto his length, the thickness stretching her in a way that made every nerve in her body tingle with delight. She was more than satisfied, and more than ready for him to get his release. She expected him to increase his speed. To pound into her like he'd talked about earlier, but what she got was cautious touching and tender caresses as he rocked them together. Joining their lips in one passionate kiss after another.

It was perfect. This was exactly what she'd wanted. They didn't need to swing from the chandelier, but she was glad he'd been willing to take it further than usual. Leaning her back as he rocked a little quicker, tugging their bodies tight together as if he couldn't bear to be apart.

He came with his lips on hers, whispering her name.

Her entire body buzzed with pleasure. She was warm and protected, and listened to.

Maybe even loved.

Maggie smiled and leaned her head on his shoulder to hide the moisture in her eyes. She didn't know what she'd done to deserve being blessed with *two* amazing men in her lifetime, but she wasn't going to complain. And she *wasn't* going to take it for granted.

She was going to hold on with both hands if necessary. Clay had taken the first step, and she was determined he would never regret it.

CHAPTER 17

Clay transferred another full wheelbarrow load from the back of his truck to where Maggie worked on her hands and knees, positioning the first of the sturdier plants into the prepared garden plots.

She smiled at him, and a warm glow pooled all over him, not just desire but, pure honest affection.

Okay, a whole hell of a lot of desire too.

"You keep looking at me like that, and I might have to take you into the garden shed," he warned.

"Scandalous." She pretended to cover her mouth in shock. "You better make sure you get such wicked thoughts out of the way before the rest of the work crew show up."

"When are they getting here?"

Maggie laughed. "In case it was a real question, Daniel said by nine o'clock." She rose, brushing the dirt from her knees before coming to stand at his side. "The project is looking fantastic."

He nodded. "It's not your typical way to build, but at least now that the exteriors and walkways are done, you can finish making the outside look pretty while they wrap the interiors."

"Do they have a lot to do inside?" she asked. "I haven't been keeping track of that part."

"Daniel said they're on schedule for August 1. I'll know more by the end of today." He pulled her close and kissed her briefly before motioning to the load of plants. "Where do you want me to put these?"

She gave him his orders, and he happily provided the grunt labour, working at her side to turn the barren landscape into what would soon be four beautiful homes.

They'd committed to helping all day while the weather was clear, but Clay was already thinking about tracking his father down. There was a long unfinished conversation that needed to happen soon.

As the sun beat down on the project and trucks rolled in with willing hands to complete the labour, Clay caught himself staring at Maggie with what had to be a goofy grin on his face.

An older gentleman paced along the brand-new sidewalk, moving slowly as he took in the activity. Clay searched for a name, finally recognizing the man as Bill Tiessen, one of the long-time locals who'd been around forever.

Maggie was working in the dirt right by the road, and she tilted her head up as Bill cleared his throat.

"Are those hosta you're planting?" he asked, poking the garden bed with his cane.

She nodded. "A bit of groundcover. We've also got other perennials to put in, plus I'm leaving room for annuals for the people who like to garden."

"That will make my Gillian happy." He stared down the row of tiny apartments, nodding with approval. "And

I like the bleeding-heart bushes—makes me think of my first house. Margaret had them planted everywhere. I used to tease her about what a horrible thing it was to come home and see these little hearts hanging on the line."

Maggie laughed. "That's my name. Is that your daughter?"

He shook his head. "Oh no, my first wife, God love her. She passed away from cancer five years ago."

"I'm so sorry."

He dipped his chin. "She was a lovely woman, and I miss her very much."

Clay waited on the edges of the conversation, ready to rush forward at the first hint that Maggie needed him, but like always, she was a trooper, although there was a touch of sadness in her voice as she carried on the conversation. "Are you one of the people moving into the complex?" she asked.

"Yes, my wife and I are looking forward to it, her even more than me, I think." His eyes sparkled. "There'll be a lot less cleaning than in our old house."

Maggie nodded. "So you've remarried?"

He smiled conspiratorially. "I should think so. When you know how good it is to have a true partner in this life, why would you not want that again?"

A crystal-clear laugh rang from Maggie's lips. She glanced over her shoulder at Clay, and he didn't even pretend to be not eavesdropping. A hint of tears sparkled in her eyes, but there was obvious joy on her face before she turned back to answer Mr. Tiessen. "That's a wonderful way to think of it."

The older man offered her a smile and another nod before chatting a little while about other plants then moving down the sidewalk and finding somebody else to visit.

Meantime Clay's brain scrolled through endless loops of *holy shit. Holy fucking shit.*

His feet might be firmly on the ground, but he was floating somewhere about twenty feet off the air. He hurried forward to Maggie and joined her on the ground. Pulled her into his arms and kissed her thoroughly while they knelt together in the dirt.

Thoroughly enough that everyone working outside of the project noticed and serenaded them with catcalls and whistles, but fuck if Clay cared.

He was in love.

He was also a fucking fool that it took until now to realize the truth. What he'd been feeling all along wasn't just *caring* for her, it wasn't just wanting to be with her, it was full-out, head-over-heels, crazy-as-a-loon *love*.

She pulled back breathlessly, eyes shining with happiness. "I don't know what came over you, but any time, I'm available."

"I'll be back," Clay promised, leaping to his feet and heading to his truck. He paused with his hand on the doorframe. "I'll get another load of plants from the greenhouse. I won't be long."

"But—" Maggie sat back on her heels and rested her hands on her thighs, shaking her head as she gazed up lovingly at him. "Go. Whatever lit your pants on fire, go deal with it. But if you're not back by lunchtime, I'll make you move manure all afternoon," she threatened, shaking her trowel in the air.

Clay left behind the beehive of activity at the habitat site and drove straight to the Thompson and Sons shop. He wasn't sure he even closed the truck door behind him, he was so intent on reaching his goal.

He rushed past Troy and Mitch who were rebuilding a fancy road bike.

"Hey. You want to get out later today for a ride?" Troy shouted after him.

"Maybe. Is Dad upstairs?"

Mitch answered. "Yeah. Also, Anna said to mention the Colemans are having a bonfire out at Joel and Vicki's tonight. If you and Maggie want to come."

Dammit. Clay spun on the spot and marched back to his brothers, well aware he was about to freak them the hell out. He got to Troy first, grabbing him and giving him a backbreaking hug before turning to Mitch.

His second brother had stepped of range and was watching with suspicion, one brow arched. "Are you high?"

A bubble of delight exploded inside Clay. "No, I just had my ass handed to me by an octogenarian. It made me realize a bunch of things, and one is how much you guys mean to me. Seriously," he said increasing his volume to be heard over their sudden laughter. "You're a pain in the ass, every one of you, but I love you."

Mitch pulled a twenty from his wallet and handed it to Troy as he grinned at Clay. "Let me guess. This has something to do with the beautiful Maggie Ward?"

"Maybe," Clay confessed, pointing back-and-forth between Mitch and Troy who placed the money in his wallet before tucking it away. "What the hell was that about?"

"Troy bet us that the day you finally realized you were in love you'd end up getting all gushy and sentimental."

Troy flashed an evil smile. "No one would go over twenty bucks though. You're pretty easy to read, bro."

"Fuckheads," Clay muttered softly.

"But fuckheads you *lurve*," Mitch repeated with a

cackle before opening his arms and tackle-hugging Clay until his ribs creaked.

Clay took the stairs to the second-floor apartment two at a time. He knocked, but didn't wait for his dad to answer before he pushed his way in and went searching.

He found him sitting in a chair in the living room, the TV on low. Keith wasn't watching it. He was waiting for Clay.

Maybe there was a better way to do this. Hell, maybe he shouldn't even be doing this until he'd officially announced his discovery to Maggie first, but it had to be said, and it had to be said to *this* man, sitting there so quietly as if waiting for an anvil to fall.

"I love her, Dad."

Keith didn't move.

Clay was about to explode with the truth of it. "I don't just mean like *I love peanut butter* or *I love summer days*. I mean I love her like she's what's pumping through my veins and keeping me alive. It's not air that I'm breathing, it's *her*, and while I can't imagine my life without you and the family in it, I can't survive without Maggie."

His father's face tightened.

"You said we were being disrespectful, but let me tell you, sir, if anything, I think this is exactly what Cam would have wanted. He loved Maggie, too, and he never would've wanted her to be alone and afraid." Clay lowered himself into the chair next to his dad and fought for the strength to finish, whispering the words. "I'm not saying how you feel about missing Mom is wrong, but there's more than one way people deal with losing their heart. And for me and Maggie, *this* is right."

His father took a shaky breath as he cradled his head in

his hands and stared at the floor. It was Clay's turn to wait. Praying that his father would see reason—

His phone vibrated, and he pulled it out to check the message.

Mags: Everything okay?

He glanced at Keith before texting back *I think so. Maybe. I love you.*

Fuck. He hadn't meant to do that yet.

There was a pause, and then...

Mags: I love you too.

Mags: Just curious. Is there a reason why we're texting this?

Clay: Because I'm a stupid son of a bitch?

Mags: LOL

Clay: I'll be back soon

Mags: OK. BTW, I sent you a pic

He would check it later. He pushed his phone back in his pocket and prepared to leave.

His father rose at the same time. His face drawn, lines sharper than usual. He took a deep breath then grabbed Clay, pulling him in for a hug. Keith's breathing turned choppy as he fought tears.

"I'm sorry. I'm so sorry," he repeated over and over.

A rush of relief mingled instantly with concern as Clay held his dad and let him weep.

Even though Clay was itching to get back to Maggie, he stayed and talked it out. Let Keith confess his concerns, his fears. Share some of the sadness he still carried after years without his wife.

Clay broke down and admitted how guilty he'd felt in the early days, fighting his desire while feeling like he was the shittiest friend ever. "But I couldn't stop wanting her,

Dad. And it tore me in two at times, but I *always* came back to doing what was best for Maggie."

His dad nodded slowly, meeting Clay's gaze. "I don't say it often enough, but I'm proud of you. I should have trusted you more. I spoke without thinking, and I'm sorry."

Clay's chest was tight, but the sheer relief that he was the only one who'd ever know about his father's moment of weakness was worth the suffering. "It's okay, Dad. We never meant to hurt you, either. Only when it comes to Maggie, doing what's right for her is always going to win. She's got a piece of my heart that no one's ever touched before."

Lingering sadness lined Keith's face. "And that's how it's supposed to be."

When Clay finally took his leave he crawled into his truck then took a moment to catch his breath. The burden he'd been carrying for weeks was gone, his plan for the future set. He felt relief, and frankly, giddy as a kid as he sat for a moment and considered how much his life had changed.

That's when he remembered Maggie's comment. He pulled out his phone, opened his messages and his jaw dropped.

She'd taken a selfie. The background was blurry but what *was* clear was the bare skin of her upper body and some fine framing of what were now a very familiar pair of tits, albeit barely covered by her peekaboo bra. "*Jeez*, Mags."

Then he put his head against the steering wheel and laughed long and hard.

Life was *good*, but there was one thing he needed to make it even better.

CHAPTER 18

C lay was acting really weird. He stood across the fire and chatted with Travis and Cassidy Coleman, the entire time his gaze lingering on her.

It might be her fault. She wasn't sure what had come over her and given her the inspiration to send him the picture. It had been perfectly safe. All the guys had gone for lunch, and she'd snuck inside the garden shed, draping landscape fabric over the window before pulling out her phone and hurriedly clicking the shot. She'd felt like a fool, but figured it was worth it to put a smile on his face. Wherever he'd raced off to in such an all-fired hurry, he came back in a far better mood. She wasn't sure what was going on, but she didn't care.

She hadn't even minded that he'd left her at the project site for an hour in the afternoon on some mysterious task. Or that he'd somehow avoided any serious conversation regarding their IMed confessions, promising to discuss it that night.

Ever since he'd picked her up for the bonfire, he'd been

super attentive and affectionate. This was one of the first moments she'd had without him by her side all evening.

Instead she'd been visiting with Katy who *still* wasn't her usual self. The conversation had finally lagged to the point that Maggie was seriously concerned. "Are you sure you're okay?" she asked, because the young woman was looking positively green.

"No, not really. I should grab Gage and head home."

"Did you want me to find him for you?"

"Would you? That would be awesome." Katy made a face. "Gack."

"I'll track him down." Maggie gave Katy's arm a comforting squeeze. "I hope you feel better soon."

Katy smiled sheepishly. "Probably going to take me a good nine months to get over it." A shot of excitement struck, but Maggie snapped her mouth closed as Katy pressed a finger over her lips and *shhhhh*ed. "We plan to tell everyone soon."

Maggie slipped her arm around Katy's shoulders and gave her a quick hug. "I'm exited for you," she said.

Katy's smile was real, but definitely queasy. "Yeah, I'm pretty excited too." She stuck out her tongue and made another gagging sound. "At least once the initial three months are over. I've got to go. Pass on my message?"

Maggie went and found Gage, laughing inside at the mix of masculine pride and concern on his face as he scurried off after Katy.

She made her way over to Clay's side, catching hold of a belt loop with her fingers. He draped his arm around her shoulders and pulled her in tight. She wasn't worried that anyone in this group was going to make a fuss—they seemed to understand how special what she and Clay had going was.

Instead of rejoining the group by the fire, he tugged her toward the trees, a flashlight appearing out of nowhere. He directed the beam of light toward the ground to guide their way.

"Are we running away?" she teased.

"If you want," Clay said. "Only be careful. These are magical woods. If you run away here, you have no idea what you'll find. You might end up crossing into fairyland, and never coming back."

Maggie squeezed his fingers tighter. "Is that one of the stories you used to tell Katy?"

"Nope. This one's just for you."

Up ahead, a faint glimmer lit the darkness. Clay led them toward it until a small arbour full of twinkling lights came into view.

Maggie pointed. "Look. There's the enchanted castle."

"Joel set this place up as a surprise for Vicki. He turned on the lights for us tonight." He guided her through the archway, and she entered a fairytale kingdom. The fact that she was there with him, that's what made it the most magical. Behind them, the sound of laughter and voices carried on the air, and a couple of guitars played in the background. They could return to the gathering at any time, but it seemed as if they'd left behind everything mundane. Right now, at this moment, anything could happen.

Clay led her to the bench in the center of the bower. The seat was made of old tree stumps; the surface carved and polished until it was smooth as glass. A pale-yellow glow covered everything like moonlight. There was more than enough room on the bench for both of them, and he settled at her side, taking her hands in his.

"I kind of screwed up this morning," he confessed. "Bursting out *things* without any warning."

"I don't think it was so bad," she corrected him. "Unless you said something you didn't mean."

He stroked his thumb over the soft inner part of her wrist, sending chills through her. "The words were exactly what I wanted to say, only it wasn't romantic like this." He motioned around them.

She shook her head. "The fact you said it makes it romantic. I think my heart just about jumped out of my chest."

Clay's lips twisted into a smile. "Speaking of surprising people..." He reached into a pocket and pulled out his phone.

She pushed it aside, slightly embarrassed. "Are you mad at me?"

"Hell, no." He waggled his brows at her. "Only I'm glad you weren't nude, and I've already deleted it. I don't want any pictures of you floating around the Internet. You're mine, and shots like that are for me to see and no one else."

"Sounds possessive." She stroked her fingers along his forearm then higher until her hand came to rest on his muscular shoulder. "I'm okay with that."

"Good, because..."

He shifted off the seat and onto his knees in front of her, and the pleasure inside her welled up even stronger. The expression on his face was so clear and determined. No hesitation. No more remained of whatever it was that had been haunting him.

"Clay?"

"My timing sucks, but what I want to say can't wait. You know that whole thing you told me about needing someone to be your partner?"

She nodded, her throat tightening

He lifted her hand to his mouth and kissed her knuckles

softly. "I want more than that. More than a partner, or a lover, or a friend. I want it *all*, Maggie. Every single thing you can give me. "

He fumbled in his pocket then blew her away by pulling out a simple single ring in a familiar pattern. It looked suspiciously like the ring she already wore—a jeweled wedding band nestled against a cluster of diamonds, and she found herself breathing slower as she fought for control. "Oh my God, Clay."

He swallowed hard, obviously nervous. "It's quick, and this might seem crazy to other people, and if I'm wrong, you let me know and we can get something completely different. But Cam told me ages ago he'd ordered the third band of your ring for your anniversary. I'd already been in touch with the shop because I didn't want them calling you, and I figured, what the hell, I'd buy it, and..." he shook his head, "...and I can't believe I'm babbling like this."

His voice shook as he slipped the ring on her finger, matching it up with the two sections she already wore. So much love in his eyes as he spoke.

"He's always going to be a part of your heart, and mine, but if you marry me, baby, I promise to do my damnedest to love you as much as he did. And I'll love you for as long as we have together, with everything that's in me. I don't want to ever forget him, or what he meant to you, so that's why this ring..."

He paused, sucked in a deep breath, then finished in a rush.

"It's you in the middle, Mags, with Cam and me on either side, loving you."

He couldn't go on, and she couldn't answer him, not with words. The only thing she was capable of was throwing her arms around his neck and clinging hard.

Tears of joy fell. It was the past that allowed her to have this present moment. There in the middle of a fantasy bower, Clay changed her future.

She cupped his face in her hands and stared into his eyes. Her caring, oh-so-careful Clay. The man she knew who would do anything to make her happy.

"I love you with everything in me," she whispered. "And I would love to marry you. And I think this ring is just about the most perfect thing I've ever seen, and that makes sense, because you and Cameron are the perfect men for me."

Clay kissed her. Long and slow and sweet, and she curled her fingers through his hair and soaked in his loving touch.

It took a while before they had to break for air, but when they did, a sigh of relief escaped him. "I swear I can't take much more of this emotional rollercoaster. Hell, I even told my *brothers* I loved them," he complained.

She laughed, "You big softy."

He lifted her hand to his lips. "A complete marshmallow, but only when it comes to you."

She glanced around at the twinkling lights, and the reflections that set the stones of her ring glittering. But the things that shone the brightest were the love in Clay's eyes and the joy in her heart. He was right. Sometime in the past few minutes they'd passed over to a magical world, and they were never coming back.

EPILOGUE

They were back at the house Clay had grown up in. Everyone had shown up so far except Troy. His brothers and sister, his best friend, and the rest who'd joined their family were lounging in folding chairs in the backyard. Tanner, who was celebrating his first birthday, sat in his high chair with more cake on his face and in his hair than he'd eaten.

As far as Clay was concerned, all was right in his world.

At his side, Maggie's fingers were linked through his where their hands hung between their lawn chairs. Len and Mitch had pulled out disks and were setting up an impromptu Frisbee golf course in the field behind the house.

Keith Thompson sat beside his grandson, leaning an elbow on the edge of the high-chair tray as he had a serious conversation about nothing, a washcloth in his hands.

Clay twirled the ring on her finger, the satisfaction in his heart rising as he caught her eye.

"You shouldn't look at me like that," Maggie

complained in a whisper as she leaned closer. "Not when we can't go home for another hour."

"I can show you the best make-out spots in the garage. Or at least the ones we kept catching Troy using. *I* never fooled around in the shop."

"Never?"

He drew an X over his chest and offered her a dirty grin. "But I'm totally willing to change that, just for you."

The heat between them wasn't fading. Every day it burned brighter and hotter as they learned more about each other. How to please each other, and how to be a couple, not just in bed, but out of it. They shared their joys and fears—they'd talked about everything from his mom to debating which house to keep. Big decisions, small ones. All of it made richer because they did it together.

On the far side of the house from where they sat, someone laid on the brakes hard enough the protesting squeal echoed into the backyard. Clay turned his attention toward the noise, curiosity rising as a door slammed shut then the vehicle raced away, gravel spraying as the engine roared.

The mystery was answered a moment later when Clay's baby brother rounded the corner, hands shoved into his coat pockets as he slowly strolled in. What appeared to be a red handprint marred his cheek, but Troy wore a cocky smile as he sauntered up to where his nephew sat.

He pulled a small football from under his jacket and presented it to Tanner. "Here you go, killer. Start practicing so you can wow them with your moves down the road."

"Looks like *your* moves made an impression on some-one." Mitch pushed past him, grinning pointedly at Troy's cheek before taking a pit stop at the snack table to grab a handful of pretzels.

Troy curled his lip. "Screw...." he glanced down at Tanner, "...drivers."

"And hammers. Maybe a few flyswatters."

"Mitch. Give him a break." Anna paced by on the other side, eyeing him curiously. "Although if there's *anything* you want to talk about..."

"Nope. Nada. Everything is fine and dandy."

Clay kept out of it. Maggie squeezed his fingers and whispered to him. "You guys really are shitty liars in this family."

He laughed. "Yeah, I guess we are."

Clay didn't know what was going on with Troy, but somehow he figured his brother would find a way to come out on top. He always had before, and if he did need help? There were a lot of people around with willing ears.

Everywhere else he looked he saw good things. Mitch and Anna, thick as thieves. Len and Janey alternately giving each other googly eyes then teasing each other like they had for years.

Katy had Gage to help her with their coming challenges.

Keith Thompson finished wiping the sticky mess off his grandson then placed the little boy on his feet, carefully keeping hold of his hands as they walked together to the sandbox.

There had been some tense moments there, but the family was intact. In fact, they were stronger than ever, and Clay had never been more grateful.

Maggie settled into his lap and draped her arms around his neck. "You're wearing the most beautiful expression."

"It's called family. Between them and you, I've got everything I've ever needed."

New York Times Bestselling Author Vivian Arend brings you a sexy and emotional series set in the foothills of the Alberta Rockies. Meet the Thompsons—five siblings with secrets and dreams. Join them as each member of this tight-knit family discovers love.

Thompson & Sons
Ride Baby Ride
Rocky Ride
One Sexy Ride
Let It Ride
A Wild Ride

ABOUT THE AUTHOR

With over 2.5 million books sold, Vivian Arend is a *New York Times* and *USA Today* bestselling author of over 60 contemporary and paranormal romance books, including the Six Pack Ranch and Granite Lake Wolves.

Her books are all standalone reads with no cliffhangers. They're humorous yet emotional, with sexy-times and happily-ever-afters. Vivian pretty much thinks she's got the best job in the world, and she's looking forward to giving readers more HEAs. She lives in B.C. Canada with her husband of many years and a fluffy attack Shih-tzu named Luna who ignores everyone except when treats are deployed.

www.vivianarend.com